KISS OF THE REAPER

DEATH IS NOT THE END

ELLIS LEIGH

Kiss Of The Reaper

EBook ISBN: 978-1-954702-33-2
Paperback ISBN: 978-1-954702-31-8
Large Print Hardcover ISBN: 978-1-954702-32-5

Edited by Silently Correcting Your Grammar, LLC

Cover by Stefanie Saw at Seventh Star Art

For inquiries contact ellis@ellisleigh.com

For all the readers

wishing for just one more chance...

KISS OF THE REAPER

There's this moment when you die.

This final sliver of time when the Grim Reaper comes to lead you through to the other side. When you are bathed in the glee he exudes at introducing another soul to his cold, dark world, and you have a split second of complete and utter fear at what lies ahead. Fear of the afterlife you have no control over. Fear of the Reaper.

But not all deaths end the same way.

And the Reaper isn't who you think he is.

This is the story of how I died…and how Death himself brought me back to life.

CHAPTER ONE

THE FIELD

"The door is there again."

"You and this door," my mother said, a light, teasing tone to her voice that directly contrasted the concern in mine. "Sarah, do you see a door?"

The cards in my head, the ones that had been showing me the future since I'd been a young girl, slowed their flipping at my mother's voice. They continued to move, of course—I hadn't known them to be very still since my death—but the speed at which they flipped decelerated, giving me a glimpse at their details. Women danced within the worn edges, scenes of life playing out on tattered stock with gold filigree trim. Pictures moving and rotating within frames. Most of the people on the cards I knew—my sisters, my coven mates, my family, me—but some I only recognized from old pictures shown to me by family. There were also ones who had no place in my memory, yet there they were, showing me choices and results, decisions and the consequences they wrought. None that affected me, but I saw them anyway. Always had.

When the cards slowed to an almost stop, I turned and looked toward the woman who had raised me. The one who had taken over when my mother had died shortly after my birth. The one I had put in the ground just months before my own death. Sarah Bishop. She glanced up from her string craft, her eyes meeting mine with nothing but kindness and acceptance in them, and shot me a wink.

"I see nothing, but that doesn't mean there is no door."

Ximena, my mother, huffed a laugh and rolled her eyes. “This isn’t some metaphysical physics lesson—if we can’t *see* the door, then there is no door.”

“But your daughter sees the door, so it exists to her. Amber, honey, where do you see it?”

I said nothing but looked in the direction of the door because I certainly did not want to disrespect my elders, even though I knew neither would see the gateway in question. No one ever did. Just me.

The door stood plain as day across the field, a dark slab with a thick, swirling pattern that reminded me of clouds carved into what looked like wood. The stone trim extended a good six inches beyond the slab, cracked and pockmarked with big spaces between each chunk and a dirty sort of flatness to the front. The sort of stone one expected to see covered in green moss as Mother Nature reclaimed that which had been forced upon her. But there was no moss, no green or brown. Not any color, really. The door stood in an almost colorless space, all grays and tonal blacks against the vibrancy of the land around it. Imposing with its size and the way it seemed to devour the colors, fading them into a nothingness that stood in stark contrast to the surroundings.

And the surroundings were quite important to the oddness of the door. Any sort of entryway might not have seemed an odd thing for me to see until one realized the three of us were sitting in the Summerlands. The land of dead witches waiting to be reincarnated to continue on their magickal journeys. The Summerlands sat bathed in bright, almost oversaturated colors. Screaming in yellows and greens, burning in oranges and reds. Our blues were incomparable, our greens so deep they stole space from dark browns and true blacks. The dreary, washed-out door didn't fit. It also didn't belong anywhere near where I sat in the vibrant, grassy field with a luminous blue sky overhead. There were no buildings around, no structures or domiciles. Nothing but nature as far as the eye could see.

And yet, there stood a door.

A door that sat cracked open just enough to get a glimpse inside, to see the darkest of the dark licking along the edges. The cryptic space beyond calling to me. Inviting me through.

"It's just so…there," I finally said, wanting someone else to see it as well. Needing someone to confirm my visions. To tell me if they felt as drawn to that opening as I did.

My fingers twitched against the red strings I'd been braiding together, stealing my attention. The thread I'd been working on had developed a bit of a flaw along the length. A tiny mistake—a bump where there should have been nothing but smoothness—but a flaw, nonetheless, in a thread meant to tie two souls together. That bobble would create a slight crack in the road to forever for the couple who would be bound together with the string once it had been put into use, a minor inconvenience that reminded the couple that even with a fated union, life would not always be easy. I should have fixed the flaw, unraveled an inch and rebraided the segment to a more perfect thread, giving them the smoothest path possible. I should have, but I did not.

Bitterness rose in my throat as I left that mistake right where I had made it and continued braiding. My own thread—the link from my soul to my fated love—had been damaged beyond repair long before I'd ever even had a chance to meet my soul mate. Had severed my connection to a man who should have been mine. I'd always known my red thread had been cut, had always accepted that aspect of my life had been ended by no fault of my own, but to see it—to know that there was actually a strand of red woven by my ancestors left dangling in my chest with a blackened and rough edge—had left me with a deep and dangerous sense of being cheated out of my true fate. A need to finally make that connection in my next life. If I chose to reincarnate.

"It is definitely there…for you, sweet child," Sarah said, her voice calm and low. Her words rolling across the space between us to push away the silence. "Just as that bump will be there for whoever is gifted with your thread."

I shot a glance her way, withering under her bright stare. Guilt roiling at her gentle smile. With a sigh, I looked down at the red fibers in my hands, at the flaw I'd left. At the difficulty I had built into someone else's love story. I ran a finger over that bump, shame and bitterness building within me. Anger, too. But those were my emotions, my feelings at how the last life I had lived had played out…and how it had ended. My feelings did not deserve to be foisted on to another.

I unraveled the thread past the flaw and began braiding a clean, perfect strand once more. Pushing down the jealousy burning up the center of my chest at the idea of another witch being gifted a whole and completed red thread. Of them reincarnating into a fresh, new body and beginning that next chance to fulfill their destiny. Refusing to allow the wickedness inside me to taint someone else's future.

"Whoever weaves my next thread had better make sure it's extra sturdy," I said, not really directing my comment at anyone in particular.

My mother answered. “It will be, for I have already requested you receive one woven by me for an extra bit of Weaver family magick.”

“You did?”

“Of course. I wanted you to have the best chance this time through.” She slowed for a moment, her voice changing. Her tone softening. “You can go back whenever you’re ready, you know. I’ll be here to welcome the others when it’s their time.”

Her words rang with truth—technically, I could choose reincarnation and go back to the realm of the living whenever I wanted to. I would receive a fresh start and a new body, a sparkling clean chance to live a full life. I would also likely lose my gifts, and I would definitely be forced to live a life without the memories of my two sisters, who had outlived me and would continue to do so. Who had been my focus and parts of my heart since our birth. The two women—two witches—who made up the rest of the Weaver triplets.

I wasn’t ready to give them up just yet and might never be, so I sat in the Summerlands with the other witches not yet ready to live another life, waiting for some sign that my turn to go back had arrived. For some sense of rightness when I thought about leaving my family behind and returning to start anew. I sat and I waited and I wove red threads for future generations that would be stronger than mine had been. Necessary work for those of us in the Summerlands. Painful but necessary work needed by our kin to help them find their fated loves.

"I can't think of another witch who ever saw any sort of door in the Summerlands," my mother said, still weaving away. She'd died when I'd been just three days old, but I'd known her the second I'd come through that very door I kept seeing. Had recognized her eyes as those of my sisters and me. Being in her presence was a gift that I did not take lightly.

Sarah—another witch I had been blessed to know—huffed. "Your daughter has talents outside the realm of the other witches, is all."

"She's always been quite powerful." My mother glanced my way, a concerned look passing over her face. "Amber, your thread is tangling."

I looked down to the red strings in my hand. The thread had, indeed, tangled. A flaw, I could see handing off, a little hitch on the way to finding a soul mate, but the tangles were too much. I would not want future generations of witchy women to have to deal with my distraction in such a way. Finding a soul mate as a witch was near impossible already, and the flaw in the thread only made that task harder. The thread had become tainted with my sour energy—it should not be shared.

"I'll burn it," I said before cutting the strings and tucking the damaged thread into my pocket. But instead of braiding another thread, I lay back in the grass and let the sun warm me. Let the cards in my head flip and twist and turn. Forward and backward through time I went, seeing friends and family and acquaintances. Checking in on some. Backtracking to others.

The door always reminded me of a death speaker named Aoife who had helped guide me through my death, so I let my cards flip until I got to that point in my life. To standing in the cold and grayed-out realm of death. I'd ended up there after my earthly death, a little lost and unsure of what to do next. A little too connected to my sisters to be ready to leave them behind. Aoife had followed me into the land on the other side of the door—the land between the living and the dead—and had helped me make it to the Summerlands. Had led me to this side of that very door.

But that day had long passed, so I flipped forward again, keeping an eye on Aoife through the years. Watching as the love between my death witch friend and her wolf shifter soul mate grew and became steady. A living, breathing force tying them together. Their soul connection beautiful.

If not a bit painful.

I always got a little sentimental thinking of Aoife. She and I would have been friends; I was sure of it and had seen it in the version of the visions that hadn't led me to my own death. We would have been linked by our opposite bits of magick, two powerful beings in our own right, coming together to balance and ground the forces within. Her death magick being centered in the earth element, my craft centering on air. My two sisters —Azurine and Scarlett—being water and fire witches. The elements in balance, the magick able to build on that stability. Our lives intertwined would have been amazing. But that connection would have to be explored in another life, seeing as how I'd given up mine.

I lay in the sun, lost in my visions, for what had to be hours. It wasn't until the warmth began to fade that the feeling of being watched began to grow, that I realized I'd been still and silent for too long. I opened my eyes, frowning up at the dark cloud swirling above me, and looked around. My mother and Sarah had left, leaving me resting in the field. Not all that unusual, but this time, not having my family watching over me sent a chill up my spine.

I was alone...but not really.

I sat up slowly, knowing exactly what I would see but still shocked at the visage before me. The door—the portal to another realm that seemed to follow me around—remained nearby, wide open and ready for someone to walk through. But this time, the door wasn't across the grassy field, sitting past a vast expanse of variegated green blades. No, the door did not stand yards and yards away. It loomed right next to me, less than five feet from where I had been resting. So close, I could feel the chill of the realm beyond leaking into the Summerlands. Could sense the weight of someone else's eyes on me. Covetous eyes. Greedy ones.

For the first time since the day I'd walked through that very door, I got a good look at what lay beyond. Just as I'd remembered, the realm inside sat dark and eerie, shadows and wisps of smoke rising from anything that appeared solid. Swirls of reality melting away and yet not. The portal offered a different reality from the Summerlands, one made up of the same space and yet altered. The horizon aligned but so very different from the view around the sides of the door.

It felt as if that portal had punched a hole in my reality and washed it out, desaturating it until only shades of black and gray remained. A spot of nothing in what should have been a riotous world of color.

Inside the door, creeping at the edges of my view, stood a deep, dark spot that didn't match with the empty field beyond. A shadow where one didn't belong. One that pulsed as if breathing, that sent wisps of black vapor rising into the air. One that seemed to be the source of the heavy gaze that made goose bumps rise along my arms.

I knew that shadow, had felt it for as long as I'd been in the Summerlands. Had feared it. The shadow watched me. It coveted and craved me. And it somehow enticed me to step through that open portal and join it in the realm of death like a lost soul. Made me want to get up and just…go. Walk out of the colorful landscape and escape into the darkness. That shadow seduced me in ways that made no sense.

I could not give in.

"Go away," I said, the power of my magick turning my words into intentions, into a spell. A gust of air blew across the field and whipped up and around the door itself, grass flattening along the way. That wind whistled as it hit the portal, weaving into and around all that stone trim. Finding secret nooks and crannies to disappear through. A wall of air making my wants clear to the shadow on the other side.

For a moment, the briefest sliver of time, I thought I saw the shadow move. Thought it sagged as if in defeat. Thought I witnessed a split second of something like emotion through that portal to the nether world beyond. I didn't see enough to be sure, though.

In the next second, with a screech like a wounded animal, the door slammed closed.

CHAPTER TWO
THE VISION

The dark, swirling cloud I had awoken under felt as if it never left, even with a bright Summerlands sky above me. Something about that moment, about waking up with the door so close, had stuck with me. Soured my mood. Infiltrated all my thoughts. I couldn't stop seeing it. Couldn't stop remembering the fear and trepidation of knowing I was being watched. Couldn't stop wondering what would have happened if I had moved a little closer.

"Have you checked on your nieces and nephews lately? Sorrel and Ginger are doing well in school, though Poppy seems to be taking another path altogether." My mother puttered around the old cabin we'd conjured, something to give us the normalcy of life on earth. Me more than her, to be honest. The afterlife had not come easily to me, so we'd developed habits and routines based on those who still lived. That included a safe space to call our own and hours of respite that we didn't actually need. Spending time in the cabin with its dark walls and soft, golden light gave my mind and eyes a break from the wild colors and vivid spectacle of the Summerlands.

Also, as I liked to remind my mother, some habits died harder than I had. A thought that reminded me of my life in the living realm.

"I've seen them," I replied, remembering flashes of young men and women living lives I'd never been a part of and the sharp smack of loneliness those images had caused. "I try to give them privacy, but they come up now and again."

"And you see them clearly?" she asked, obviously excited about something. "I can't see the same level of detail you can, but I like to know what they're up to."

I swallowed hard and nodded, ignoring the uncomfortable prickle along my skin. "I can. They all grew up so fast."

Which was why I didn't watch them as much as my mother did. The lack of a sense of time bothered me, and the way my visions jumped felt disconcerting. One second, little Sorrel had been a babbling baby with unfocused eyes and chubby cheeks. The next, he'd been walking across a stage with a gown and mortar on, accepting a degree from a high school I'd never been to. Pudgy legs became long and lean, while those first toddling footsteps became powerful strides across schools and places of business. I missed the middle moments, the times when the unimportant events happened. The meat of the lives continued to live without us. I missed the best parts, and that hurt. Still. Because while visions were nice, they weren't actually the same as being present in the moments being lived.

It would be nice to go back, just for a day, just to see my sisters and their children. Aoife had come through from the land of the living into the realm of the dead to lead me to the Summerlands. For the briefest of moments, I wondered if I could do the same but in reverse. Just…walk through the door.

My mother, halfway through making a pot of tea for the two of us, gasped and dropped the hot kettle. Scalding water splashed everywhere, but she didn't notice. Didn't jump or scream in pain. My mother stood stone-still, eyes completely unfocused but looking straight ahead. Locked in a vision, for sure.

"Mom?" I approached slowly, knowing how absorbing visions could be but also concerned—she never lost herself in her gift the way I did. "It's okay, Mom. It'll be okay. The vision will pass."

My mother started to shake her head slowly, her wide eyes going slightly red and her cheeks flushing. For just a moment, I could have sworn I saw sparks glittering at the edges of her dark hair, but then she opened her mouth and whispered a single word that stole every bit of my attention.

"Scarlett."

My long-dead heart, unused and unneeded for decades, dropped. Scarlett—my youngest sister and the last triplet born. A wild child from birth with the gift to control the element of fire in ways even the most powerful witches envied. She lived on an island in Northern Michigan and ran a boarding school for homeless witchlings, collecting the children who had been tossed out by their parents for having too much or not enough power. And apparently, she was in trouble.

I reached for my mother's hand, needing a little guidance to find the right spot in time. Bringing my sight in line with hers. The cards flipped immediately in my mind, so many futures laid out before my eyes. So many lives being lived without my presence. The cards stopped at a scene that I couldn't quite grasp, the image like something from a television show.

The card on top showed me the boarding school for sure, but the entire building and surrounding area looked wrong. The image in my mind appeared grayed-out and deeply shadowed, as if all the color had seeped from that little patch of the earth. Dehydrated and moody, as if the entire island had been absorbed by the land between the living and the dead. I searched for Scarlett in the windows of the big house I'd never physically entered, trying so hard to ignore the way my vision blurred and went staticky whenever I sought more detail, beginning to recognize the wisps of black vapor rising into the air.

"No," I whispered, gripping my mother's hand tighter. In the vision, the wind howled, and what looked like dead leaves blew across the wide front porch. Autumn on the island, a time of shifting from tourist season to rest. Very few locals lived on the island year-round, so once the tourists left, it should have been quiet and safe. Should have been a time of peace. Should not have been disrupted—

And then I saw her.

Lying on the porch floor, right outside the front door. Dark hair with bright red streaks like fire slowly fading to gray as it fanned out across the wood planking. That flame-like hair stood out as the only hue against the gray background, the only impregnation of color in a world of shadows.

The hair…and the blood. So much blood.

"No!"

The vision shifted suddenly, the cards reversing themselves to show me another scene. This time, Scarlett was alive and bright, running through the snowy woods with a green scarf around her neck and a smile on her face. Her own soul mate, a shifter named Shadow who carried the spirit of both wolf and tiger, plodded along behind her in his wolf form. The two playing what looked like a happy and fun game of hide-and-seek.

One more shift in the vision, another reminder of what was to come. One last vision of my vibrant sister dead and gray on the floor of her boarding school. The flame within her snuffed. Her magick lost.

I didn't need guidance on what the visions meant. Option one, option two. Dead or alive. Scarlett's path had not been chosen yet, decisions that would determine her fate not yet made, but she didn't have much time left to make those choices. Death was coming.

I took a good look at the scene playing behind my eyes, focusing on every detail. I saw no defensive wounds, no sign of a fight. No burn marks or scorches around her. Perhaps someone she had known had done that to her, someone in her trusted circle. A friend could soon betray her. Or maybe the attack had been mystical in nature—something not of the ordinary stealing her life too suddenly for her to react. It was impossible to know.

The wind howled again, dead leaves definitely flying up and around the windows. An indicator of time that crossed dimensions. Even in the Summerlands, we experienced the seasons. As witches, the equinoxes were especially meaningful to us, and we celebrated them just as we had while alive. The dead leaves indicated Mabon, the second celebration of the harvest season. We were still in Laghnasadh, or August Eve—the first harvest—though that would be ending within a matter of days as we rolled through toward Mabon.

The leaves danced on the air again, my own element giving me one last chance to home in on the timing of this tragedy. I watched each leaf with interest, paying particular attention to the details. Green centers, brown edges—not completely dead or dried. Early Mabon for sure, which meant…

"Days," I whispered, my mouth going dry with the knowledge of how soon Scarlett's life could be over. "We only have days."

But our skill, our precognition, had given me the gift of those days. Scarlett's death had been in the future, which meant it was something I could stop. I could play a game of cat and mouse with Death to stop him from taking a life deserving of more time. I would just have to challenge him from his side of the playing field, from the land between that of the living and the afterlives. I would have to face off against Death on his own turf to save my sister.

I'd beaten him once before—I could do it again.

"It's not happening." I shook off the vision and came back to the little cabin, letting go of my mother's hand and racing across the room. One swipe, and everything on the kitchen table went flying, eventually crashing to the floor. Ignoring the cacophony, I grabbed the salt and climbed onto the table, settling with my legs crisscrossed. Salt in hand and names of the elements on my lips, I cast a quick and crude protection circle before diving into my visions at full speed.

"Amber?"

I shook my head, not wanting my mother to attempt to distract me. "Element of air, of breath and life, I call on your guidance and speed. Give me sight. Help me seek and find the one I need to stop this travesty. My sister cannot die—not today, not this week, not this winter. Fill me with your power and help me stop this."

My mother stepped beside me, standing clear of the salt. "What are you doing?"

"I'm sending a message." I closed my eyes tighter, hanging on to the sides of the table as my visions raced past me, cards flying in a way to almost make me sick with the movement.

Just hang on, Scarlett.

"She won't see it," my mother said, her voice fading as I dove into my visions full force. "She doesn't have our gift of sight."

"No, she doesn't." The visions stopped, a steep hillside with thick pine trees reaching toward the sky surrounding me. "But Percy does."

"Who is Percy?"

I shushed her, needing to focus hard to find him. Needing stillness and concentration to work my gift this way. I rarely tried to sight the future so aggressively. I'd done it before, during the time leading up to my earthly death as I had fought to shift the futures around me so my sisters and my disconnected soul mate could find their happiness. So they could live long, fulfilling lives.

Death had lost the fight for their souls and taken mine instead, but apparently he wasn't done with us. He thought he could take my sister.

He was so very wrong.

"Scarlett—"

"Not now, Mother."

I sank deeper into my vision, reaching further into my mind to find the man I'd met right before I'd died. The little precog who had helped me with setting up a battle scene that would lead to my death. Not knowingly, of course; I'd made sure to hide that particular future from him. At least until the very end when I couldn't hide any longer. But Percy had been a good partner, and the two of us would have been excellent friends. He would help me save Scarlett. I knew it. I trusted him to. I just had to find him.

A cabin in the woods appeared up the hillside from where my vision had chosen to establish visual connection, smoke rising in a dance from the top of the chimney. The place looked homey and warm, with rocking chairs on the porch and a colorful door. A bright-blue door and a light-blue porch ceiling—haint blue. The colors needed to keep the spirits of the dead away.

Definitely Percy's house, and probably his best friend—the death witch Aoife—had painted that ceiling for him.

"Here we go." I shoved my visions forward, throwing every bit of energy I had behind them. Making a connection to the living that stretched my bones and stole my breath. Making the reality in those woods pulse as I gritted my teeth and reached toward that cabin.

Percy came racing onto the porch with wide eyes that carried far more wrinkles than I remembered, looking around as if he felt my presence. As if he knew I needed him. I had no doubt that he did, but I wasn't done yet because the need technically was not my own. It was Scarlett's.

"I am so sorry about this," I whispered, the words hard to say. The physical side of me strained to the max. One last mental shove, one last bone-crushing push in my mind, and I shifted my focus to the scene of Scarlett's dead body. Threw it toward him with a scream that left my throat raw and inflamed. Knowing that strong of a vision would overwhelm him but having no other choice.

I wailed as the pull between realities—mine in the Summerlands and his with the living—broke, as my powers built to the point of breaching the wall between us. The cards I had grown up seeing in neat piles and clean shuffles exploded in my mind, disappearing along the edges of my vision. My joints ached and popped, my body twisting and burning as if I were being ripped in two. Still, I didn't stop. I pushed that vision forward, using every bit of magick I had ever been taught. Not pulling back until I saw Percy fall. Until two men came running onto the porch, calling his name. Until they lifted him to a sitting position. He pushed them off, crawling across the floor to the edge of the porch. Staring straight at me through the railings.

"Amber."

My name on his lips gutted me, the catch in his voice too painful to ignore. I broke, sobbing right there on the table. Something about him remembering me so many years after my passing shifted my emotions. Jerked them suddenly from one side of the spectrum to the next. So suddenly, I couldn't hold the connection. The last thing I heard before the vision went dark was Percy's voice saying, "I need to call Aoife."

My head hit the table as my body collapsed, the breath I technically didn't need rushing out of me. My mother spoke words I could barely hear, pacing along the side of the table where I lay, but I couldn't make sense of them. Not really. I was too tired, too far past the point of my own reality, to try to understand her words. Still, I turned my head toward her. Cried and stretched and forced my exhausted bones and muscles to move. To fall. To surrender to gravity once more.

That was when I saw it.

The door.

Outside, just past our own front porch. Sky swirling dark and gray above it, winds whipping the grasses as if a storm brewed nearby. So close, that door. So wide open. I felt it then, the need from within. The pull.

The door—and whatever lurked on the other side of it—was coming for me.

My mother's own cries continued, gaining volume. Words piercing my haze. Something about *not working* and *try again*. But my head was too foggy, my body too weak. I didn't have the strength to focus, didn't have the energy. I could not fight against the weariness that had infiltrated my entire being.

The last thing I saw before unconsciousness took me was the shadow moving on the other side of the door. Watching me.

Waiting for me.

CHAPTER THREE

THE WITCHES

I woke with fire in my joints and every inch of my skin pulled too taut, as if I'd stretched more than just my magick. The pounding inside my head reverberated like a pulse, continually punching me behind my eyes and ears. I'd experienced a magickal rebound before—an echo of the energy I had sent out coming back at me—but nothing like this. Nothing this painful. Even the cards in my head, the images that had kept me company most of my life, sat still and silent. As if they knew a simple flip or flop would send me over the edge.

I lay prone on that table, the salt I'd used to cast my circle rough against my cheek, until breathing no longer took effort. I lay still until the pain stopped dominating my every second. But lying facedown in the mess I'd made and not knowing what was happening with Scarlett wasn't going to get me anywhere, so eventually, I pushed up to a kneeling position, fighting gravity the entire way and keeping my hands on the table until the world around me stopped spinning. Once that position no longer hurt, I pushed myself off the table and onto my feet. Standing. Wobbly and weak, but upright.

The pain in my head intensified, but that didn't stop me. Couldn't. I had to know if my plan had worked. My cards remained dormant, meaning I had no glimpse into the future. My mother would, though. Her gift may not have been as strong as mine, but it would work. She would be able to see. I just had to find her, had to will my body to move. Had to pull myself together and just…walk.

"This is going to hurt," I whispered to myself before taking a deep breath and beginning what felt like the long trek to the front porch to find my mother. She wasn't in the cabin; that was easy enough to determine without stressing my body. She had to be outside. So, I moved away from the table—stiff and limping and so very tired—and I made my way to the door. Almost crying at the weight of it but slipping through the opening to the vibrancy beyond its wooden protection.

My mother sat in the grass field just past the edge of the porch, staring off at the horizon as if meditating. Still and quiet, just like the cards in my head. A bad sign.

"Mom?"

"Scarlett won't make it," she said before I could even reach her. Before I could say a second word or ask a single question. "Your sister won't survive the week."

Fire erupted inside me, burning unlike any I had experienced before. Building and blowing and razing every piece of me from the pit of my stomach to the tips of my fingers. My joints reignited, though this time not in pain. In unadulterated fury. In pure rage.

"No," I said, my word harsh and direct. A bullet piercing the otherwise quiet space.

"I'm sorry. I know you tried, but…" Her head bowed, moving slowly from side to side.

I opened my mouth to speak but snapped it closed. There, on the edge of the forest past the field of tall grass, stood the door. The portal between the Summerlands and the land of the dead. The entrance to Death's playground and, coming from the other side, the way into the Summerlands. That door did nothing to quell my anger, but it did pique my curiosity. Was Scarlett's impending death why I'd been seeing it? Was the door present as an omen of another Weaver sister soon to be residing in the Summerlands?

"Why?" I asked, needing so much more information. Wishing my cards would begin their flipping already so I could *see*. So I could figure out how to help Scarlett. How to once again stop Death himself.

My mother shook her head, shoulders sagging and body rolling forward. Looking as if she had completely surrendered. "I can't see what's coming for her, but something is. The strait between the island and the mainland is freezing early, and because of the ice shutting down the ferry service, no one will be able to get to her in time. Your friend is trying hard, but it won't work. Nothing will work."

I stared at the door, wondering if my mother finally saw it too. Knowing my own sister would eventually be coming through that portal. I could almost picture it—wild black hair dyed with red streaks blowing in the breeze, loud mouth likely already yelling the second she appeared. She would fill the Summerlands with energy and light, bring fun back to my life. Bring joy. I'd missed my sisters like nothing else. They had been staples in my life from birth, and being away from them had been so difficult. But this wasn't right.

"It's not her time to die."

"No, it's not." My mother sighed, sagging further, wrapping her arms around her knees as she gave in to her grief. "Someone is going to take her fate away from her and end her life. That's not the way a witch should return here."

A firestorm of anger exploded in my mind, burning away any doubt or fear that could have existed. Burning away my exhaustion, too. I stared at that door with hatred running through my veins, with a storm of magick and mayhem brewing inside me. Aoife the death speaker had brought me through to keep me safe from Death, had protected me in that plane of existence between the living and the afterlife. I was no longer allowed to go through the door because I wasn't meant to be there.

My sister wasn't meant to be there either.

Nor was she meant to be in the Summerlands, yet someone planned to send her here with their thoughtless actions.

Yes, Death lay on the other side of that door in all his dangerous glory, but right in that moment, I had a feeling Death should be the one afraid of *me*.

Aoife had gone there to save me. It was my turn.

My mother gasped, but I had already headed for the cabin, pure determination pushing me past the residual pain from my magickal rebound. I stood tall and sure, my stride strong, putting together a plan with every step forward. Making the decisions I needed to so I could save my sister.

"Amber, no!"

I kept moving, not allowing the fear in her tone to slow me down. At least not until she caught up with me and grabbed my arm. I spun and glared at her, my head high and my path chosen. Giving her all the ammunition to make her case.

"Tell me I won't make it back."

My mother, a precog just like me, said nothing. And I knew, I *knew* that I might not. That decisions would need to be made along the way that could change the overall outcome. My cards weren't showing me much yet, had only just barely begun to lift and slide a little, but they would. They would be there to guide me through the land of Death. They would be there to help me save my sister.

I reached for my mother's hand, knowing this would be hard for her. Sensing her fear. "I'm the only one who can save her."

"Death is out there," she said, her voice small and choked. "It's not like the Summerlands in his plane. He'll take you and feed on your soul, and you'll never be reincarnated again. Your magick will die with you."

I huffed and spun again, rushing inside. Sarcasm dripping from my words as I asked, "You're worried about my *magick*?"

"Yes, your magick. The Goddess—"

"The Goddess already killed me," I yelled, smacking my hand to my chest where my tattered and torn red thread lay damaged. Shredded by Death himself. "The Goddess and Death took my soul mate from me before I was even old enough to understand what I would be missing out on and then set me on a path to have to give my own life for his. They started this."

"Amber, I know—"

"You don't!" I slammed my hands on the table, sparks flying at the contact and the ground beneath my feet rumbling. A physical manifestation of my temper brought about by my powers. "I died so my sisters could keep living full lives. I gave up everything for them. No one gets to step in and take their lives now, not after all I've done. Not after all I've lost."

My mother stood silent, watching me with sad eyes. Every ounce of her spirit broken and tucked away. She had been dead a long time—had lived in the Summerlands for what on earth had been decades as she waited to be reunited with her children. As she watched over us from afar while her coven had raised us. And while I could empathize with how difficult that must have been, she had been safe while we had not. She did not get to tell me how to defend my sister.

"I can do this," I said, not backing down. "I *will* do this."

She bowed her head, nodding gently just once, then sighed. "Fine. Just…give us a minute."

With that, she rushed outside and off the porch. I stood at the entryway, staring after her. My feet itching to follow her even though I had my own plans and needs to fulfill. Thankfully, my body knew better than to turn away from that opening because within seconds of my mother rushing through it, a thick, red light burned and whipped across the sky like some sort of energy beacon. As the light danced against the clouds above, a thunderous boom broke the silence of the Summerlands. The cabin shook under the sound, magickal implements tinkling and trembling as if about to be brought to life.

But the true show wasn't inside with me; it appeared outside with my mother. With the people who began to appear in the tall grass, rising from the earth as if summoned. I stepped outside, unable not to follow. To ignore the draw of the power my mother gave off.

"Who are they?" I asked, staring in awe as more and more people—all women—approached the cabin.

My mother stared into the field, stoic and strong. Holding on to that red light as if it were a whip. Directing it across the sky one more time before letting go and watching it dissipate into the ether. "They're our ancestors and past coven mates. Anyone in the Summerlands who has a link to the Weaver magick is coming."

She wasn't kidding—ten women, fifteen, twenty. They kept appearing, walking slowly toward our cabin. Approaching the very porch I stood on. A few I knew or recognized. Most I did not. All gave off an aura of peace and care, of support. All practically vibrated with magickal energy. These were my people, my family. My tribe. My true coven. And they had come to help. I had never felt so relieved, supported, and under pressure all at once.

The first woman to make contact was sweet Ardessa, my great-grandmother, who looked so much like an aged version of my sister Azurine in that moment that I nearly cried.

"Here, child," she said, handing me a rucksack decorated with an owl holding a key in its claws painted on the front. "Carry this with you. I packed a few special things to help you on this journey."

"It's beautiful," I said, admiring the embroidery, the details throughout the lines that made up the image.

"Owls are a symbol of death, Amber. Their hoot is an unlucky omen to most, but they can be particularly helpful where you're going. Keep this close."

"I will." I took the bag, feeling the magick inside the fabric. Feeling the love and strength of being responsible for something so vital to the Weaver line. But as I lifted the bag, something inside shifted and clinked. I met the eyes of Ardessa, wanting to question her.

My great-grandmother gave me a wicked sort of half smile and a shrug. "Little spell jars. Things you may need that offer protections for our kind. That's all."

I had a feeling *that's all* was a massive understatement, but I knew better than to push for more information. "Thank you."

Sarah approached next, her soft smile and worried eyes hiding nothing. She handed me an amulet with a large black stone at the center. Obsidian, if I remembered correctly.

"I raised you the best I could," she said, her voice strong even as her hands shook. "Use the magick I helped you grow, child. Use every bit of it so you come back to us."

I grabbed her hands, clinging to the matriarch from my former life. "I will. I promise."

She stood whispering a protection rite as I placed the amulet around my neck, then gave me a smile and a nod before disappearing back into the crowd. The third witch gave me a small crystal vial, letting me know it held a supply of Florida Water, also whispering a blessing before releasing my hand. The next handed me a chicken foot and some other small, unidentifiable bones, her magick a force I could feel pouring off her. She bowed her head and whispered words of sight and knowledge, asking the Goddess to help me find my path. When she finished, she grasped my hand a little tighter and reminded me that the bones would tell me all I needed to know.

On and on it went, witches of all kinds, magick makers of all races and practices, coming together to offer me what they could. To give me their tools for protection and strength. A full multigenerational coven of witches, standing in the grass lending magick to one member.

All while the door sat open mere yards away.

Finally, the last woman approached. This woman wore a haggard old body, her light blue eyes surrounded by wrinkled skin but sharp as a hawk, her white hair hanging almost to her ankles. A woman of great power and knowledge. I could feel it.

As I watched, the woman shifted forms, growing younger. Middle-aged, perhaps. Her hair turning dark like mine, her skin smoothing, and her body growing more voluptuous. Feminine beauty in human form. And again, another shift. Younger still. Blond hair this time, skin tight and clear, body slimming slightly. Watching me the entire time. Not breaking eye contact. At least not until she glanced down to my chest.

To my annihilated red thread.

"Oh," I said, understanding hitting me like a brick. This wasn't a witch—this was someone so much more powerful. The maiden, the mother, and the crone that together made up the Fates. A personification of the Goddess weaving the threads of life, dispensing them, and cutting them when our time on earth had come to an end. Tying us to our other halves along the way. This woman had power unlike any I could even imagine. And she was looking right at me.

As she shifted back to the form of the crone, she raised a gnarled and spotted hand, tapping a single finger against my breastbone right over my thread.

"No one beats Death forever, child."

I took a deep breath and raised my chin, feeling the weight of my body pressing into the ground. Pulling on all of my strength to even find words to address such a being. “I’m not looking to beat him forever. Just this time.”

She chuckled, shifting to her mother form. Looking a lot like my own mother but without the golden-brown skin. “You have always been a challenge, dear Amber.”

“I never intended to be.”

Her laugh rang across the field, the breeze picking up as if to join in her joy. “Remember this, love—not all villains are enemies, and not all heroes are friends.”

She held out a strip of fabric—dark and worn, the edges frayed. Without effort or thought, I lifted my arm, allowing her to fasten the strip around my wrist. I stared down at my hand, a tingle of power spreading from the fabric. When I looked up again, eyes likely wide from the knowledge of the gift I had received, the young figure had replaced the crone. The maiden staring back at me.

"May your ancestors guide you and keep you. Blessed journey, my child." She gripped my hand a little tighter, rubbing her thumb over the back of it. "Don't forget to grab a sweater before you go. It's cold in the land of Death."

My hand burned where she'd touched it, a sigil forming on my skin as if etched. A runic shape I had learned to draw as a child—an overlapping set of greater than and less than symbols with a line bisecting them from top to bottom. Old magick that had evolved in the modern world as something of legend, as symbols sold in trinket shops. My runic sigil was no trinket, though. It filled me with a sense of love and strength. The warmth of her protection soothed my internal rage, refocusing my energy and giving me a confidence I had been missing.

My cards exploded into motion in that moment, the future laid out before me in parts and pieces, still needing me to choose my path to be solidified. My trek into another plane of existence would be difficult, and there would be many decisions to make and opportunities to fail, but I had a chance. I saw Scarlett laughing and alive in the snow as the cards danced in my mind, which meant I could do this. I could save her.

I had to save her.

"Thank you," I said to the Fates, raising my voice so the rest of the witches heard me as well. "Thank you all for coming and for offering your gifts. I feel protected by your magick." I tucked the last of the gifts into the rucksack, grabbed my favorite rust-colored cardigan from the chair by the door, and strode off the porch, heading into the tall grasses. Walking straight for the door that no one else had been able to see. The portal to the land of the dead. The only way I had to reach my sister on any level.

The need to enter overcame me, the pull of what lay beyond irresistible, but still, I stopped before entering. Standing before the doorway with one hand on the strap of the rucksack thrown over my shoulder, I turned to look over the assembled witches one last time as my long skirt whipped around my legs in the breeze. My mother stood at the front of the group, eyes on mine. Sadness radiating from her. I could not ease that, though.

Nothing to bring her joy unless I came back. And I would. So, I raised my hand in the air, and I gave her a simple wave, absorbing the gift of the support of this coven of women.

And then I stepped over the threshold.

CHAPTER

FOUR

THE SHADOW

Cold. The Goddess had been correct—the land of the dead was very cold in comparison to the Summerlands. Dark, too, but not quite black. The land of the living, just…not. Gloomier, more sinister, and colder, yet with all the landmarks and locations of their regular world. The land of the dead appeared like the land of the living in structure but somehow reversed. As if the colors had been switched to their opposites then desaturated to a barely-more-than gray.

It took me a long moment to adjust, to accept the vision before me. A really long moment. Even glimpses through the door and the splotchy memories of being lost here once before had not prepared me for the land I had entered.

"If this is Kansas, I'll take the Land of Oz instead."

A wind whipped past me, chilling my ankles and making the hem of my skirt flutter. My bright and colorful skirt—apparently the land of the dead had failed to affect me. The bold skirt was likely a bad choice of clothing for such a place, but my clothing tended to match my surroundings, and the Summerlands sat under the brightest sky, always warm and comfortable and dynamic. Not here. Dark clouds blocked the majority of what should have been a sunlit sky, and the trees stood as white sentinels in the shadowy forest. Wisps of what looked like smoke rose from every surface that moved, almost like a thin but black fog that spread with motion instead of temperature. Perhaps a result of heat moving in the cold air. Perhaps Death sucking the life from anything and everything in the plane.

Creepy didn't begin to describe this world, but that couldn't stop me.

Tugging my cardigan tighter to ward off the chill, I hiked my rucksack a little higher on my shoulder and started walking. The cards in my head sprang to life, flipping and spinning as I surveyed the area and decided on a path. Without the sun, finding my way north would be harder than it should have been, but the cards would tell me. The future depended on my making the right decisions, which meant making a lot of wrong ones first. Two turns and a quick spin, then I spotted it—a card with Scarlett's flame-like hair dancing on the breeze, with snow in the background and a feeling of joy attached to it. A future with my sister alive.

I strode in the correct direction, taking advantage of the flat land to gain some time. I had no idea how long the trek would take me, but I assumed it would be far. I had died outside of Chicago, and Scarlett lived on Mackinac Island—walking that far had to take at least a week. Of course, I had no idea if I'd entered the land of the dead at the same location as my death. I could have been in Canada or Arizona or Poland. I could have been just a few miles away from my sister or halfway around the world. But the cards flipped and showed me glimpses of red-streaked hair blowing in the breeze instead of flat and gray against the floor. That meant there was a chance for Scarlett's survival if I just kept moving.

So, I kept moving.

It didn't take long for the grayness of the world to make me feel out of place. I stood in that place in full color—rust-colored cardigan, bright patterned skirt, and dark hair practically luminescent in the desaturation of the landscape around me. I definitely stood out, which made me a target. Fear intruded into my thoughts, and sounds began to invade my focus. Small sounds—a crack here, a shuffle there. The noise someone makes when they're trying not to make any. The sounds of someone following me through the woods. Likely because of the sounds, I began to feel the weight of someone watching me. Began to notice the hair on the back of my neck standing up as if I were in danger.

"Stop it, Amber," I said to myself, tugging my cardigan again and keeping my stride as steady as possible. "There is nothing to fear."

In the culture of witches, speaking something into the universe could help manifest it. In the land of the dead, the worlds I had always known but in reverse, speaking those words caused the universe to prove me wrong.

A shape suddenly appeared above me, a dark and wailing wraith screaming across the sky. I froze for just a second, but that was enough. The black figure dive-bombed me, flying around my body, almost close enough to touch. Winds kicked up long-dead leaves and ephemera from the grassland, blurring my vision and making it harder to breathe as my panic grew. The wraith encircled me, and I had an impression of black robes and gray skin, of white teeth gnashing in some sort of warning. I couldn't get a visual on the face, though. Not a good one. The shape seemed humanoid, but the energy the wraith gave out definitely felt threatening.

Without thought, I yanked my rucksack around and in front of my chest in a protective hold and reached for the obsidian amulet around my neck.

"You cannot do me harm!"

The wraith flew upward, rejoining the gray sky and screaming like a banshee, as if my words had held weight. As if they'd worked in some way. The creature's retreat didn't mean the fight had ended, though. That much I knew, so when I saw my chance to escape, I took it, which meant running.

I could hear the screams from behind me as soon as I reached the tree line, recognized what sounded like distress or anger as the creature followed me. Didn't matter—I kept running, kept ducking behind trees, kept trying to put distance between me and that thing.

I had just slid down an embankment, twisting my ankle slightly on the way down, when the wraith appeared before me once more. Nope, not *the* wraith. Another wraith, because the screaming one remained overhead and circling. This one seemed to float before me. Staring at me.

Perhaps sizing me up. Perhaps waiting for me to make a mistake, which seemed likely. Being outnumbered by undead flying spirits would cause anyone to choose wrong.

"By the Goddess." I backed up, unsure of what to do. Cards flipped through my mind as I contemplated every option of escape I could think of, pictures racing past my internal eye. Every option led to my death. To Scarlett's. To failure. A deep, burning pain settled in my chest, and my breathing became almost labored as my body went on full alert. I kept trying to back away, kept trying to think of something—anything—I could do so the cards could show me the way through this. I couldn't fail so soon, couldn't lose my own soul and my sister because of two creepy ghostly things. That just…

Well, it pissed me right off.

"Get away from me!" My scream echoed in the woods slightly, and both wraiths sort of went still. Staring at me. Watching me like an animal in a zoo. Okay, good to know—they seemed unused to being yelled at. I clutched the obsidian amulet tighter, running the fingers of my other hand over the fabric band around my wrist. Calling on the fae, the Fates, and any deities I could think of to give me strength and volume, to keep me safe. To infuse my words with intentions. My magick was all I had left.

"Element of water, cleanse me now, carry me through, enhance my vow." Terrified but putting faith in my ancestors and my powers to protect me, I turned to my left and took my eyes off the wraith before me. Fighting to keep the tremors racking my body from showing. "Element of fire, join me here, charge my words, burn my fear."

I turned again and froze, terror dripping down my spine like ice water. A dark shadow had been standing behind me, a mere few feet away. Close enough for me to see each and every wisp of smokelike vapor rising from its shape. Close enough for it to have reached out and taken a bite.

"By the Goddess…"

I choked as the creature cocked its head, the shape cloaked in black and impossible to truly see. But it was big and humanoid, tall and thick and as dark as Death itself. Perhaps Death had arrived. Perhaps the end had come for me.

But as I stared, the cards began to flip again, showing me in motion. Playing a scene of me running through the woods on an endless loop. The image shifted suddenly, giving me a glimpse of hair like fire trailing after a woman running through the snow before cycling back to me and my journey through the woods. I stood totally dumbfounded by this possibility, giving the shadow enough time to creep forward. To lean in and breathe me in before I even realized it had moved.

"You are loud, little witch."

The sound of his voice—because that creature had used a decidedly masculine tone—and the feel of its breath scraped along my skin, causing goose bumps to rise up and down my arms. Scratchy and deep, somehow entrancing yet terrifying, his words might have made a lesser woman cower. But I was nothing if not my mother's daughter.

"I will not lower my voice."

He cocked his head again, the movement animalistic and sharp, and released a grumble almost like a chuckle or a laugh. I had just moved my leg to take a step back when that grumble turned deeper, darker. Turned to a full-blown growl. I gasped and shifted my weight back, twisting my ankle again and falling to the forest floor as he swept his arm in my direction. I thought for sure I'd feel a connection, that he'd land a hit to my head or face, but no. He moved his arm in an arc and roared toward the sky, his black hood falling back. His actions sending the wraiths straight up into the sky, where they disappeared into the darkness above.

Leaving me alone with him.

My ankle throbbed, but I climbed back to my feet, not wanting to put myself in a vulnerable position against him. The cards were still flipping, though. Still showing me Scarlett's hair in the snow even though I had not ended up running through the woods. They confirmed that I remained on the right path still. How that could be, I had no idea, but I held on to that hope as hard as I could.

The man before me didn't meet my eyes when he dropped his head forward once more and turned in my direction. He never looked high enough for that. Instead, he stared at my chest. I had a moment of feminine rage—of assuming he dared to objectify me for my breasts—before I realized in the land of the reversed, some things were more visible than others. In the land of the reversed, my tattered red thread sat bright and practically glowing in my shadowy and hollow chest.

A fact that left me feeling oddly vulnerable under his intense scrutiny.

"Stop staring," I said, tugging my cardigan around myself to cover what was none of anyone else's business.

The man looked up, eyes finally meeting mine. A scream bubbled up inside me, nearly impossible to hold back, as I saw beneath the shroud he wore.

Black eyes, flat and dead, seemed to devour me on the spot. Gray skin covered his harsh face, hazy and not at all solid along the edges as if somehow dissolving into the ether around him. His shroud moved almost of its own accord, as if a living entity resting on him instead of being a cloth he wore. He stood huge and thick and scarred, looming over me, with an air of malice unlike anything I'd ever felt before radiating off him. The man exuded danger, a true threat in every sense of the word.

And he continued to stare right at me.

I tried to scramble back, but my ankle buckled as I moved, causing me to stumble hard. The man did not attempt to catch me or follow me, leaving me to fall as he watched. I didn't fall, though. Not completely. I caught myself on a tree and managed to stay upright, to keep my eyes on him. To try to move away.

As I retreated, he took a single, terrifying step forward and said, "I am not a threat to you, little witch."

"Liar," I spat. "The Fates tell me otherwise."

A statement delivered with conviction even though the validity of it seemed unlikely at best. The cards continued to flip in my mind, to play out the future, to show me red hair and snow. They didn't show me anything of myself, though. Nothing with me alive or dead, nothing of my future whatsoever. They did nothing to help me determine if the man could be trusted or not. I chose not, just in case.

But the man didn't advance on me as I rose to my feet. Instead, he kept his distance, and he did something I couldn't even have imagined as possible. He transformed his physical shape right before my eyes.

His skin went from gray and wispy to paler and almost solid. His eyes from deep, dark black to a piercing dark blue. Everything about him became more distinct and true, less ghostlike. Less terrifying. He might have even been considered handsome to some who enjoyed the look of a man who seemed able to break your spine with his fingers. Because even though his physical appearance changed, his size did not. The man was a boulder in comparison to me—crushing, hard, and impossible to move.

But then my visions changed, showing me once more. Showing him at my side. They adjusted to his new appearance, only showcasing this more appealing version of him in the future.

My brain had obviously taken a turn down an unhealthy trail.

As I stared at the man before me with the strong jaw and the piercing eyes, the cards began to flip even more aggressively and show me more of my own future. Small moments in time—ripped clothing, harsh hands around my neck, my own scream as something dark and horrible bit down on my flesh. All with that man before me by my side. All with him in the picture.

All without context to know if he had planned to protect me or sacrifice me.

“What is this?” I grabbed my head, closing my eyes and looking inward. “Why are you putting these images in my mind?”

"I am not responsible for what is happening in your head, witch. That is all on you."

"Lies." I stumbled as I tried to move away again, grabbing hold of a tree to pull myself to my feet. "Who are you?"

He stood stock-still, staring at me. Almost seeming to be waiting for something before finally saying, "I am the reaper. The collector of souls and the navigator for this plane of death. I am Grim, and I am not responsible for whatever is upsetting you."

I was about to call him a liar again, was about to start scraping at my scalp to stop the endless visions of the two of us together, of his cruelty toward me, when a scream from overhead made my body go cold. A shadow flew across the ground, the black robes of one of the wraiths passing right in front of me as the creature completed a swoop.

Grim didn't pause this time. He raced at me, picking me up in the middle of a stride and running through the woods while tossing me over his shoulder. The future continued to play out in my head, making me dizzier than being carried upside down ever could. A future filled with demeaning moments but companionship. With something that resembled a relationship filled with what looked like violence. With moments I knew were impossible. And yet, as he ran, I saw flashes of red hair, which meant I was still on the right path. Every future had him with me and red hair paired with snow, every picture a reminder of my end goal but with him lurking in the corners.

I could see no way past him. No way to stop the visions. No chance of escape.

To save my sister, I had to stay with Grim.

To save Scarlett, I had to cozy up to the reaper himself.

CHAPTER FIVE

THE PLAN

Grim ran a lot farther—with me thrown over his shoulder like a sack of potatoes—than I would have ever thought reasonable. Still, I didn't move or fight. Didn't argue or try to talk my way out of whatever this master escape plan of his was. Instead, I kept my mouth shut and let the cards flip, looking into the future as deeply as possible. Ignoring scenes of Grim and me to focus on Scarlett. This entire trip was about Scarlett.

Eventually, Grim came to a stop in a meadow of high grass surrounded by tall pine trees with black, wispy tops that almost seemed to scrape the sky. He practically threw me down onto the grass, his breaths coming fast and hard as he loomed over me. As he forced my eyes away from the trees above to his dark, inky blue ones.

"Why are you here?"

I flinched at the volume and depth of his voice, the pure rage in his tone. The heat rising within my chest burned bright and painful, indistinguishable from the flame of embarrassment or self-hatred. Of humiliation for showing such a being a single spot of weakness. I would not make that mistake again.

I made sure to keep my voice solid and sure as I said, "My sister needs help."

"The living help the living," Grim said, spitting his words as he began to pace away from me. "The dead stay where they're supposed to be."

"The living couldn't help her, so I came through the door to try myself in this realm."

He froze, standing statue-still for a moment before making an entirely too slow spin to face me once more. The expression he wore, the absolute blankness on his face, made my skin crawl more than a scowl or a frown could have.

"You could see the door?"

"Of course." But even as I said the words, the fact that I could see the door while others in the Summerlands had never mentioned it stood out. The memories of telling my mother about it and her responding with a blank look sank in quickly, igniting something that made me ask, "Was I not supposed to be able to?"

Grim dropped into a crouch, his black shroud falling open, revealing the dark, almost denim-like pants beneath. His thick legs bulged under the pressure of the stance, spreading that black fabric wider. No shirt covering the hint of his grayish, muscled abs. He may not have been standing at his full height, but he still took up so much space.

Grim leaned forward, cutting off my view and making me sneak a look at his face. He inched even closer, once again attempting to loom over me, his shoulders seeming to grow wider as he placed one fist on the ground for support. A warrior ready to fight, waiting for some sort of sign of aggression. For war.

"Could you see through it?"

His cold and emotionless tone sent my instincts flying. The ancestors whispered through my brain, the cards responding to the sound as if it were a physical force like a breeze blowing through my mind. Calm infused my soul, and a sense of warmth enveloped me. A sense of rightness. This moment held importance, held gravity in regard to the Weaver magick. This was not a moment to lie.

"Sometimes," I said, pausing to lick my lips. Watching as his eyes darted to follow the motion before returning to mine. Deep pools of blue burning as they tried to consume me right there on the grass. I had never been more obsessed with a man and yet terrified of him at the same time. "Shadows, mostly. Wisps of fog—" I raised a finger, letting it follow the path of the smoke that never stopped leaving his skin "—or whatever this is."

He continued to stare, stabbing me with his gaze. Pinning me in place as he waited for more. As if he knew, as if he sensed that I was holding back. As if the ancestors were whispering to him, too.

I bit my bottom lip lightly, needing that slight shock of pain to recenter myself. Craving it. Shivering as his eyes again darted to my take in my mouth.

“What else, witch? What aren’t you telling me?”

And yet, I paused, silent and still. Waiting on something. Needing to take a breath before I whispered my final admission.

“I could feel someone watching me. The weight of their eyes on my body. I knew—I always knew—that someone—”

The cards in my head bolted into position, flipping recklessly and stealing my words. I felt myself go limp, felt my eyes unfocus as I gazed inward at the deck shuffling madly. Forward and backward this time, future and past. Showing me glimpses of my own reality, of the shadows through the door. Of the details I hadn’t noticed and the shapes I had chosen to ignore. Opening the truth wide for me as an image of glowing blue eyes appeared in my mind.

By the Goddess...

"You've been watching me."

Grim huffed and rose to his feet, pacing once again. Long strides eating up the land and heavy footfalls vibrating through me. They were the only sound he emitted, though. He remained silent but for his tread, unspeaking. Not confirming or disputing my statement.

I moved as if to rise to my feet, wanting to feel on the same level as him in some way, but the second my right foot touched the ground, my ankle gave way and I fell back with an embarrassing squeal.

Grim was there in an instant, one hand on my leg and the other set beside my hip as he leaned over me. Crowded me. Invaded my space. "What is it?"

I sniffed, trying to get past the throbbing pain now radiating up my leg. "My ankle. I must have twisted it worse than I thought."

With hands far gentler than I could have imagined, Grim tugged my wrists until I released my ankle. His rough skin burned slightly as it ran along my own, the lack of any heat in his flesh oddly soothing. He pulled off my shoe and dropped it absently to my side, completely focused. His fingers scraped against my skin as he lifted my long skirt, his soft touch in total juxtaposition as he ran his thumb over the bone on the outside of my ankle. Examining me.

"How long has it hurt?"

"I didn't realize it did."

"Do you remember hurting it?"

"I tweaked it a couple of times trying to escape those…wraith things."

He grunted in a form of approval. "You've likely sprained it."

"At least it's not broken. I can walk on a sprain."

"Sprains can be worse than broken bones when it comes to an ankle. You'll need to take care of it." He pushed off the ground, stopping once he'd risen to his feet to stare down at me and frown. "Stay here. Don't move."

The instinct to nod came hard and fast, the feeling of accepting him and trusting him to care for me. I should have run, should have waited for him to disappear then taken off and tried to hide. I should have done a lot of things that I did not do because the cards never even hinted that I needed to. They seemed to trust Grim—the reaper—which meant I would as well. For now.

Grim raced off into the trees, coming back a minute later with what looked like mud in his hands. He sat before me, tugging my ankle up onto his thighs with his dirty hands. The mud wasn't really mud—it was something warm and sticky that smelled like pine and the earthy aroma of freshly turned soil. It smelled…alive. Odd, considering we were in the land of the dead.

"What is that?"

"Something you shouldn't know about." He kept his focus on my ankle, rubbing the sludge over my joint and onto my foot. "But it will help. Do you have bandages in that bag?"

"I'm not sure—I didn't pack it." I moved as if to bring the bag forward, to bring it between us, but Grim grunted and shook his head.

"It's fine. I'll make do." With that, he tugged a piece of blackness from the shroud that seemed to be a living, breathing part of him. A strip of fabric—gauzy and so very dark—tore away from the main garment, almost defying gravity as it appeared to dance around his fingers. He took that fabric and pressed one end into the mud before beginning to wrap it firmly around my ankle.

The second it touched my skin, a chill ran up my spine and I shivered. "What is *that*?"

Grim shook his head, still focused on my ankle. "Cloth. It will help support the joint so you can walk."

But that wasn't just cloth, and he knew it. He also knew that I knew it. He simply wasn't going to tell me the truth.

"Where is your sister?" he asked out of the blue.

I glanced up from where he had been wrapping, staring at what was essentially the top of his head. He certainly wasn't returning my gaze.

"What?"

"Your sister. You said you came through to help your sister. Where is she in the living realm?"

"Mackinac Island, Michigan. She runs a boarding school there for witchlings who were abandoned by their families or covens."

He nodded, done wrapping but still staring at my ankle. "That's a long journey."

"She's worth it."

He finally looked up, once again seeming to pull me in with nothing but his stare. Smoke rising from all around him. "The Keres sisters won't give up hunting you. They won't let you escape."

I cocked my head, my brow pulling tight. "The who?"

"The specters that flew over you—your *wraiths*. They are the bringers of death and devourers of souls. They won't like you being here with that nice, tasty essence still in place." He reached forward, bringing a finger to my chest. Nearly touching me right in the spot where I knew my red thread lay abandoned and frayed. "This will be especially delicious to them. They won't be able to resist hunting you."

Fear was a funny thing. It could either freeze you in place or make you run faster than ever before. It could instill a sense of hopelessness that crumbled your very soul or a determination unbreakable from the outside. Fear may not have been a good motivator, but it could gas up your motivation more than most other emotions.

My fear might as well have been high-octane racing fuel.

"My sister needs me to survive. I will not give in to fear."

Grim rose to his feet, his motions jerky and tight. The energy rolling off him shifting into something that felt violent and dangerous as his shroud fell to cover him once more. Fog rolled in across the forest floor, making the grass beneath me nearly disappear and chilling me down to my very core. Grim seemed to be almost absorbed by the misty smoke, fading in and out as he took a step back into the darkness. Going wispy with every retreating motion.

"You're brave, little witch," he said. "An idiot, but brave. Good luck on your journey. You're going to need it."

And then he was gone, absorbed by the mist that rose and swirled, that blocked out the sky for a moment before finally beginning to dissipate.

Leaving me alone and injured in the middle of a meadow. His touch a memory. The piece of his shroud around my ankle pulsing with a magick not my own.

By the Goddess, what had he done?

CHAPTER SIX

THE AGREEMENT

A true witch needed very little in the form of accoutrements. Amulets, herbs, books, and possessions made the job easier, of course, but only the witch's innate power called to the elements and communicated with the deities. We *needed* nothing, but a good walking stick made from a branch found on the side of the road sure came in handy when that healing took longer than we wanted it to.

"North. I just have to keep moving north." The walking stick added a clicking sound to my cadence, one that I worked to keep even and rhythmic. Step-clickstep-step-clickstep. And while I walked, I watched the cards spin in my head. Watched the visions of the future play out. Desperately seeking red hair in the snow instead of grayed-out and on the floor. I saw my sister alive and happy, but only occasionally—nothing more than mere glimpses within other less important sights. My own humiliation, dark and dangerous tunnels through the earth that both intrigued and terrified me, an afterlife spent in conditions not like those of the Summerlands. A monster of a man tormenting me throughout eternity.

"I release the negative thoughts that do not serve me," I said, focusing on the cards and on manifesting some good luck and health. Unable to forget the part of Grim's shroud wrapped around my ankle. "And I welcome new ways of healing. I release the negative thoughts…"

My whispered chant continued, my manifestation shared with the universe. The magick would come through for me—I knew it. Had faith in it. I just had to keep my intentions clear and my desires specific. And I needed to keep moving.

I ignored all the visions involving myself and focused on my sister, walking on the ankle Grim had helped to make sturdy but with my stick as support. Relying on more than just him, on something I had taken from the earth to help me heal. A talisman of sorts, much like the trinkets and jars in my rucksack that clinked with every step. Step-clickstep-clink-step-clink-clickstep. My ankle holding me up but still painful. A chink in my armor, for sure.

I leaned into the urge to move faster, to chant louder, to solidify my plan and save Scarlett's life. Between the absolute hunger to do whatever it took to save my sister and the feeling of being watched, I wasn't stopping anytime soon. And yes, I knew he remained out there. I could feel Grim's eyes on me. Sense his presence in the shadows. He lurked like a specter in the woods, a shadow of malevolence waiting for me to screw up and make myself vulnerable again. That wouldn't be happening.

"Faster. I just need to walk a little faster."

As if the Fates themselves had heard my words, I broke through a stand of trees to find what looked like a road. Four lanes of concrete with a patch of tall, dead grass beyond those before another four lanes of concrete. A highway, for sure. This wasn't a drivable road, though. In the reverse, there were potholes the size of medicine balls and sinkholes with no bottom to be seen. Cracks and fault lines sent thick pieces of concrete larger than any man skyward, their sharp edges stabbing toward the sky. The entire surface seemed an invitation from Death himself, but it was a *road*, and it ran what looked like a north–south trajectory, which meant it likely would lead me in the right direction. I needed to trust in the Goddess to lead me where I needed to go.

"I release the negative thoughts that do not serve me." With a deep, bracing breath, I hobbled up the embankment leading to the concrete, wrenching my elbow on the ascent. The pain didn't stop me, nor did it linger. My healing manifestation worked overtime, keeping my body strong. Giving me the strength to continue. By the time I crested the top and set my feet on the hard surface, any sort of ache or twinge disappeared from my consciousness.

From the tree line, the road had looked dangerous. Standing on it, seeing the destruction and pitfalls laid before me, it looked absolutely heinous. It also looked like a shot to speed up my trek.

"One step at a time." I whispered the words to myself, closing my eyes just for a moment to focus on the element of earth. To feel her slow but ever-present pressure both beneath me and vibrating through my walking stick. I took a deep breath, needing my powers to guide me. I would be relying heavily on my intuition—fed by my connection to the element of air. The only thing standing between me and failure was my magick. So, I focused hard, and I chanted my intentions and my gratitude in my head, and I allowed my power to build within me. Filled myself up with good Weaver magick that I knew would help protect me. I grabbed the strap of the rucksack on my shoulder, giving it a jerk to make the contents clink, ran my finger over the strip of fabric around my wrist—the one the Fates herself had provided me—and brought the obsidian amulet around my neck to my lips for a simple kiss to its shiny surface. I prepared myself, and then I took my first steps on the road.

The cards flipped and rolled in my head, stealing my attention and making me pause for the slightest moment before I started to move again. Faster this time, taking large, quick steps with my walking stick for support. Because on the cards, clear as day, bright red hair blew in the breeze with snow flying about, the channel between Mackinac and St. Ignace visible in the background. Scarlett, alive and well, remained at the end of this road. I just had to get to her.

Step-clickstep-step-clickstep. The pattern played out like a song, like a fisherman's shanty. Giving me a goal. *Keep the rhythm, keep the beat. Don't slow down.* But I eventually came to a raised crack I couldn't easily cross without moving far off my intended path. I had to pause and almost tiptoe around the behemoth stone, slinking past it on the edge of a sinkhole I refused to look down into. The rhythm changed as I crept, the beat slowing. I couldn't use my walking stick either, so my footsteps became more of a tap-tap-tap-tap as I traversed along the edge, breathing deeply and not looking down into the black abyss. Following what little flat concrete I could find to move past the giant fissure.

Tap-tap-tap.

Click.

I froze, looking at the walking stick in my hand. The one that had definitely not touched the ground. The wind blew past me, the rustle of the trees the only other noise. I shook off the sense of unease, slowly making my way past the last of the crack. Sighing in relief when I reached solid ground once more. I adjusted the walking stick in my hand and took a step.

Click.

Once more, I looked at the stick, the one I had not yet set down. The one definitely hanging in the air at my side. Click was not clink, so the sound wasn't coming from my rucksack either. Which meant…

A chill rose up the back of my neck, goose bumps forming along my arms. That sense of being watched, of a presence monitoring me, increased. The energy felt different, though, darker and harsher than before. Colder. I took a shaky breath and slowly, so very slowly, turned on my heel to look back across the hellscape I'd just passed through. There, slipping up and out of the sinkhole I'd just performed a balancing act across, came a deep, dark shadow of a form. Floating, wispy gray smoke rising from the shape. No face or eyes visible, but definitely staring right at me. And the teeth I knew too well. Those gnashing white teeth.

My brain stuttered and spun as the realization hit me—those teeth chomping down had been the clicks. A Keres sister had found me again, but this time, I had no Grim to scare her off.

The instinctual need to flee exploded within me, but the pulse of the earth below my feet tempered it. The elemental energy of Mother Earth grew around me, responding to a witch in need. Had fire presented itself, I would have raced as fast as my damaged ankle would have allowed, same with air. But the power of earth did not move as quickly as her fire and air sisters. The energy she shared full and strong but slow-moving. The cards flipped again, showing me the image of Scarlett still alive and looking out over the water, which meant I was on the right path even with the danger before me. Slow and steady. That would be my way forward. My way to safety, or whatever constituted that in the Reversed.

I took a deep breath, breaking out into a cold sweat as I turned my back on the wraith, and began my normal pace once more. Step-clickstep-step-clickstep peppered with clinks from the rucksack. Moving away from that which could steal my soul, not even giving the creature the respect of my attention. I kept moving, kept focusing on the pulse of the earth below me, kept following the spirit guides whispering words of support in my ears.

That didn't stop me from throwing out a few protection spells along the way, though.

"I invoke my personal shield. No danger or ill befalls me. I am safe within its protection. I invoke my personal shield..."

Over and over, I whisper-chanted the words, building them into part of the rhythm of my walking. Growing the power behind the syllables with each utterance. But then a sound unlike any I'd ever heard before screeched through the air, something dark that scratched at my nerves. Something that made the words stumble out of my mouth instead of flow. Laughter. The demon behind me had started laughing. That did not bring me comfort.

"I invoke my personal shield. No danger or ill befalls me. I am safe within its protection."

I continued forward, chanting a little louder. Refusing to give in to the fear when the earth pulsed so perfectly with my words. This was the right decision—what I needed to do. I had the elements supporting me, had the power of my ancestors pumping through me. I would not be taken down by this wraith. I would not—

A wraith dropped from above directly in front of me, stopping me in my tracks.

The edges of her flowy black garment fell across my arm, the tickle of the fabric making me want to scream. Similar to Grim's own covering—that I still had a piece of wrapped around my ankle—the dark and tattered fabric chilled me to the core and twisted my stomach painfully. Dark magick lived in that cloth. The type summoned by malicious forces. The type that turned a person's soul black with hate and anger and negativity.

As I watched and considered options, hoping the cards would show me how to proceed, the creature let out another screechy laugh. This time, being so close to me, I saw her mouth open. Saw the rows of white teeth split and a shiny, black liquid begin to roll over them. Thick, viscous, and so dark it seemed to absorb the light, the oil-like substance dripped down the bottom of her face and over the garment she wore. Like honey off a spoon, it seemed to defy gravity, holding on and stretching farther and farther and farther until it finally fell to the concrete. Until it landed with a sizzle and burned a hole through the stone.

"By the Goddess…"

Another screech-like laugh sliced through the air between us, and I returned my gaze to her face. Her much closer face. The space where her eyes should have been captivated me, locked me into place like prey because they weren't there. Not really. Just a flat darkness where eyes should have been, a shadow of what I expected. She floated closer, close enough for me to smell the acrid, burned odor from her open mouth. To feel the shroud around her tickle my flesh. Close enough to sense the silence coming from within a body that had been dead far too long. Too close, yet I could not make a single move to escape. The cards had stopped spinning, my brain freezing as panic rippled through me. I saw no way forward or back. No escaping the thing that seemed to be slowly wrapping itself around me. I was trapped, unable to think or move. Totally contained. Totally—

No, my witch.

The whisper drifted through the air on a gentle breeze like a lover's touch to my cheek, the band on my wrist tightening almost imperceptibly. A reminder from the Goddess of who I was and the power within me. That contact, that slight bit of pressure, reset my brain. Gave me the keys I needed to restart what the wraith had shut down.

I wasn't stuck. I was simply restrained by her magick. And I had my own to fight back with.

"By the Goddess," I said again, louder this time. Pushing my energy outward and visualizing myself breaking free of whatever hold the wraith had on me. "You do not get to control me."

With an instinctual purpose, I held up my arm—the one with the strip of fabric tied around it—and bent my wrist so I had the palm of my hand facing the sister. A stop symbol, but also a power move to amplify the magick flowing from within. Words in a language I had never heard nor spoken bubbled up inside, escaping on a voice that wasn't mine at a volume I couldn't even begin to comprehend. Translating in my mind as if I already knew their meaning, as if I had spoken them a thousand times before in past lives lived long before my last one. And perhaps I had, because the conviction in my tone could not have come from a woman who didn't know what she was doing or saying. My ancestors had come to my protection.

"I invoke my personal shield. I am a witch of the Weaver line and a daughter of the Goddess. My body is protected. My heart is protected. My mind is protected. I am defended against attack and misfortune, thus am protected against evil and pain. I send your ill intentions back threefold. It is so."

The wraith snapped her jaws closed and flew backward, a low grunt escaping from her as I continued to push forward, as I took a single step in her direction. Hand up, palm out, words rolling off my tongue. I focused hard on the invisible link to my ancestors, the magick within that they had gifted me, and let them do with my body what they saw fit. I gave myself over to the Weaver witches past and present. Surrendered to them. And it worked.

Sort of.

As I chanted, the wraith laughed again and flew higher. Not giving up but not moving closer. At least not until it reached a pinnacle above, then dove through the air straight at me. Witchcraft, elemental magick, and ancestral guidance could not overpower my instinct to flee in that moment, the memory of that black ooze burning through concrete too raw to ignore. I ran as fast as I could and as well as I could on my bad ankle, hanging on to my walking stick in case I needed to swing it like a bat. I raced off the road and headed straight for the trees, hoping against hope the branches growing strong and thick above me would block the wraith from her current position of power. Wishing for anything to help me, to save me, to guide me down the right path so I could escape the fate nipping at my heels.

As if in answer to those prayers, a shadow appeared before me. Barreling toward me through the very trees I had sought shelter in. I assumed I had been found by another wraith, my heart dropping as I accepted that something worse than death was likely about to happen. But when the shadow reached me, it didn't stop. It didn't even pause. Instead, it flew right over me. Passed me. Heading right for the wraith instead of battling me. It…

Looked more familiar than the wraith herself.

"Grim."

As I watched, shadow Grim slammed into the wraith, the two black forms melding and spinning and wrapping around each other. Fighting a battle in the sky. I found it impossible to tell them apart, to determine who had the upper hand at any given moment. At least until one screeched and flew upward, disappearing into the overcast sky. The other—the Grim shadow—landed on the grass not five yards away from me, crouching as he touched down with a force that shook the earth. He immediately lifted his head, those dead, black eyes of reverse Grim meeting mine. That angry jaw tight and locked.

The feeling of danger only increased as I trembled under that look.

"Grim, I—"

He didn't speak, didn't wait to hear my words either. He stormed my way and grabbed my arm, his grip tight and painful. Not stopping for a single moment, he dragged me across the grass and back to the concrete road, ignoring my pleas to stop and not appearing to care as I pulled and smacked at his hold. When he finally had both of us on the road, he handed me my walking stick—the one I must have dropped at some point—and pushed me away from him.

"I told you the Keres sisters would not let you through."

Anger unlike any I had ever felt before burned through me, adrenaline fueling my temper and residual ancestral magick shoring up my confidence. "And I told you my sister needed me."

"Is she worth dying for?"

I laughed, the sound off-balance and slightly manic even to my own ears as I swung both arms out wide. "I'm already dead, remember?"

Grim froze, staring at me. Black eyes fading to that deep blue and gray skin warming slightly. Just enough to appear almost human.

"No, witch. You're in-between. Your Summerlands offer you reincarnation, a shot at a second chance to return to the realm of reality you call the living. You won't get that here. If they capture you, if they drain your soul, there is no way back."

Instinctually, I reached for the red thread in my chest. The broken, damaged part of me. The driving force behind my first death.

"I gave up everything for my sisters to find happiness, and no one gets to take that away from them."

Grim stared at my hand, his face locked, his expression one of rage. An ominous, painful energy poured off him, billowing against my legs. The entire world of the Reversed seemed to still, seemed to grow darker as if under an eclipse.

Finally, he turned and looked north, releasing the energy he had been brewing. "Mackinac is a three-day trek along this road and then a boat ride across the strait. I can get you there."

The wind picked up, the whisper of the trees a reminder. A warning of sorts.

"At what cost?"

Grim looked over his shoulder at me, eyes darkening once more. "For a favor to be returned later."

"What kind of favor?"

"Whatever I choose."

"That's a sucker's deal."

"It's the only deal you'll get, witch. Otherwise, I will leave you to the Keres sisters."

I tried to force the cards in my head to spin, to show me the right path, but they refused, remaining silent and still in Grim's presence. Only a single card dared to show itself, appearing on the side of the stack to show me a familiar image from a traditional tarot deck.

A tower, burning at the top, a bolt of lightning the cause. Two people fell from the great height—one male, one female. The tarot had never been my preferred tool of divination, but I knew enough to understand the message being sent. No matter my decision, chaos awaited me. Destruction and rebirth. The tower looked mighty and solid, but the structure had been built on an unstable foundation, making it untrustworthy and dangerous. But that card also supplied hope with its lightning bolt shooting straight down through the crown—an image meaning energy flowing through the universe. And the twenty-two points of the flames meant even more. Twelve zodiac signs and ten points of the tree of life. The card, while verifying that a dangerous and sudden upheaval had arrived in my life, suggested that no matter my choice, divine intervention would always be with me.

This wasn't a moment the ancestors and elements wanted to be a part of.

This wasn't their decision but mine, one I would have to live with the consequences of for whatever was left of my non-life.

I was on my own.

I glanced down to see that spot on the concrete —the one made by the black goo from inside the Keres sister's mouth. The hole in the earth she had caused.

My decision was not easy but necessary.

"Fine," I said, closing my eyes for the briefest of moments so I could concentrate on the pulse of the earth beneath my feet. Needing that reassurance before I gave myself over to the monster in front of me. "I'll go with you."

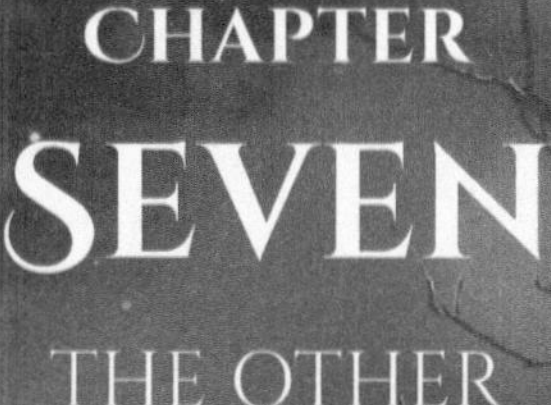

CHAPTER SEVEN

THE OTHER

Walking was no easier with Grim skulking beside me. In fact, my ankle hurt more than it had before the Keres sister had shown up to attempt to…I didn't even know. Eat me? Drain my non-body of my soul? Dissolve me in their oily oral secretions?

I really had to not think about *that* ever again.

"You're limping."

I moved my head as little as possible, side-eyeing Grim. "Yes."

"Why?"

"I hurt my ankle, remember?"

"I remember, but I wrapped it. It shouldn't hurt anymore."

"Well, it does."

Without a single grunt of warning, I went airborne. Grim had a hold on me, moving me as he pleased and without my assistance. I yelped as I flew in an arc over top of the man, but the movement didn't stop, and he certainly didn't release me. Not until he had me firmly on the ground with both legs sprawled before me, my long skirt bunched up to my knees, and had taken up the position of kneeling at my feet.

"What are you doing?"

He grunted and grabbed my leg, the one with the bad ankle. "Checking my work."

"You should have asked."

"It's *my* work."

"It's *my* ankle."

"That doesn't matter."

I was about to argue back something that I was sure would have been really witty and made a great point, but at that moment, he ran a hand up my leg. Far up. Like *all the way to my knee before bringing it back down* up. His touch felt far rougher than a human man's would have been but gentle for such a beast, and with that thought came something I had not been prepared for. Neither was the moment when he pulled my leg upward and my skirt fell, exposing even more of my skin.

"Hey." I tugged the fabric down, attempting to cover myself as Grim pulled my leg higher, bringing my ankle to his face.

A face wearing a wicked smirk. "Nothing you have there is something I haven't seen before. It's not as if you're plated in gold, witch."

My brain stopped working, and words tumbled from my mouth without thought. "But you're dead."

"I wasn't always," he said, huffing in what seemed like a sarcastic sort of way. "I've seen it all before."

I found myself almost angry, riding the edge of hurt at the idea of him all alive and being with others. I probably should have been even more insulted, but…he had a point. Not a good one, but a point.

A point I most certainly ignored as I argued, "Just because you've seen plenty doesn't mean you get to see mine."

He kept his eyes on my ankle, kept his hands running up and down my calf as he said, "Seen yours too."

I felt my jaw drop and was about ready to yank my ankle away from him when he tightened his grip, massaging my calf with thick fingers that dug deep into the flesh. A deep tissue massage by the Grim Reaper himself. I nearly fell backward with the pleasure radiating from that pain.

"Oh, that's—"

"Feel good?"

"Yes. Thank you."

"You're welcome."

I sighed, sinking into the ground as my body relaxed. Focusing solely on the way Grim's touch eased the muscles of my leg. By the way his hands held so much power and yet could be gentle enough to heal and not hurt. The color difference between us stood out in that moment —my skin a golden tan under his grayish flesh. The brightness of my skirt battling with the tonal blacks of his coverings. I could have stared at the juxtaposition of us and focused on the quiet of the moment, but eventually, Grim broke his silence.

"Why are you here?" he asked, his tone softer than ever before.

I couldn't make sense of the words at first, too busy dealing with the deep, rhythmic sensation of him kneading my calf muscles. Why it felt so good, I had no idea, but it was nearly enough for me to be willing to strip naked right there and let him—

Card flips, red hair with snowflakes floating above, the start of a turn of her face.

"Scarlett." The whisper was one I couldn't control, and it caused Grim to look up at me, his eyes bluer than ever before as his hands stilled. The sudden loss of the massage righted my brain and gave me a moment to say, "My sister. Her name is Scarlett."

"The one on Mackinac Island."

"Yes, she needs me."

"You mentioned that." He returned to his massage, moving his attentions down and rubbing the muscles just above my ankle, making me groan softly. "But why risk your soul for her?"

"She's my sister. If someone threatens one of us, they get the rest of us."

"So, there are more of you heading to help?"

"No." I shook my head, my brow furrowing. My gut clenching as if I had just been reminded of something important. "Our other sister is still alive. I wouldn't want her involved. I would never put her life at risk."

He stared, frowning, obviously not agreeing with my logic.

The urge to explain myself could not be contained. "Do you have siblings, Grim?"

His gaze dropped, his eyes refocusing on where his hands were rubbing my skin. "Yes."

No explanation, no details, and a shift in his tone that indicated the conversation was over. "Well, then perhaps you can understand. My sister needs me, so I'm on my way to her. I will not allow her to fight alone."

He grunted but didn't say a word, still focused on the way his hands moved over my flesh. Something that fascinated me as well, which was why the flash of shadowy darkness moving out of the corner of my eye caught me so off guard. I jerked as the feel of someone watching me bathed me in an anxiousness I could not control, my head twisting hard to look over my shoulder. I jumped when the darkness moved again, trying to pull my leg away from Grim as a gasp escaped my lips.

"Hold still, witch."

"No. There," I said as I pointed. Grim looked up to see the same thing I did—a figure draped in black, not a Keres sister but cloaked much like Grim, stood a hundred yards away. Energy pulsed from his form, making the world around him seem almost hazy. Making my eyes hurt to even watch him. He watched us, though—that, I could feel. There was no denying the chill up my spine. No fighting my instincts that knew we were being watched.

Grim growled a low and deadly sound but didn't rush to do anything. Instead, he set my leg down slowly, carefully, then offered me a hand. "On your feet."

"Shouldn't we be running?"

"No, but we *should* be on our way."

"But the thing—"

"The man over there is no threat for now. He won't hurt us, though he'll likely follow." He mirrored me as I finally stood on my own, placing my walking stick in my hand and crouching down so he could look me directly in the eye. "Do you trust me?"

The cards in my head flipped faster, more violently, pictures of him lording over me, of him restraining me in dark, dangerous places. Pictures of him approaching with his teeth bared and the mist rising off him like steam. Did I trust him?

"Not in the least."

He froze as if surprised, as if he had expected a much different answer. He recovered quickly, though.

"Fine, but you need to listen to me anyway. We have to walk. Now."

So, we walked, and I dealt with the low buzz of panic that raced along my skin every time I noticed the shadowed man trailing along behind us. And I tried my best not to think about the tingles left on my skin from where Grim's hands had spent so much time and energy. It had been a number of years since I'd been touched by a man—if he even was a man. A *number* of years even before my death and move to the Summerlands.

That had to be why his touch on my flesh had made me tingle so. I could think of no other reason for me to be remembering the feel of his hands all the way up and slightly over my knee. None whatsoever. I just needed to convince my traitorous brain and reincarnated libido of that.

"Tell me about the cards," he said unexpectedly, causing my thoughts to do a sort of restart. All the cards stuttered to a stop and fell facedown in my mind, their energy quiet and wary.

"Sorry?"

"You talked about the cards in your head and seeing the future of your sister. Tell me about that."

No visions popped up, no warning or show of how my answer would affect the future. Something didn't sit well with me, though, so I went with an instinctual answer.

"No."

He turned my way, frowning. That heavy brow pulled down. "What do you mean, no?"

"What does anyone mean by the word no? I mean, no, I will not tell you more about the cards I see in my head. I've already shared too much, and you've shared nothing except that you were once alive and saw a lot of women's legs and… beyond. So, no."

"Do you want to know about the women whose beyond I have seen?"

"Not in the least."

"Then I do not understand the problem."

Yeah, neither did I. Didn't mean I wasn't going to stick to my guns and keep my mouth shut, though.

We walked for a good stretch of time, both of us silent. Just the step-clickstep of my footfalls and the nothingness of his. The way he moved without sound unnerved me, but I kept walking because only forward motion was going to help me save my sister. Walking. Moving. Not giving up. Not thinking about a Grim in the living realm.

About what he might have been like, what he must have looked like. Nope. Not thinking of any of that.

I had just reached another giant crack, one that made my skin go hot at the thought of what might be hiding in those black depths, when I realized Grim was no longer beside me. I spun, a frantic sort of panic exploding through me, to find the man standing ten feet behind me with his arms crossed over his broad chest.

A statue, unmoving.

“Why aren’t you walking?”

He shrugged one boulder-sized shoulder. “You refuse to answer me.”

“About what?”

“The cards,” he said. “You won’t tell me about the cards you mentioned.”

“So?”

“So, then I refuse to walk with you.”

“You promised me you’d get me there.”

"I *promised* nothing. We made a deal."

"Is this the favor, then? To help me make it to Mackinac, I have to tell you about my abilities?"

"No. This is just something I desire to know."

The absolute fire of anger sparked deep within me, frustration at the power imbalance I found myself in fueling the blaze. "Your desires have nothing to do with our deal, Grim. I have a sister whose life hangs in the balance, and you agreed to help me reach her."

"Tell me about the cards."

If I weren't so afraid of attracting the attention of the shadow man or the Keres sisters, I would have screamed. "That's not fair."

"Nothing in life is fair."

"We're not alive. We're dead!"

He went stock-still for a moment, a brief second in time where he might as well have been a picture of himself, and then a sound unlike any I'd heard before broke the still air around us. A deep rumble, as if the earth herself shook. As if pressure had built up somewhere and finally begun to escape. As if—

"Are you *laughing*?"

Grim nodded as the sound grew louder, ducking his head as if trying to hide his expression. I could only stare at him, shocked beyond words. At least for a moment.

"Are…are you laughing *at me*?"

Suddenly, Grim blinked out of sight then reappeared directly in front of me. Close enough to touch, to smell the warm earthiness of him, to feel the cold radiating from his form. My entire body locked itself into place as he loomed over me in all his reaper glory.

"What are—"

"Yes, I am laughing," he said, his voice a thick stream of letters and syllables tweaking my nervous system in ways that were flat-out wrong. "I laugh because you're funny, witch. Because no one has ever spoken to me the way you do. You're unique, and that fascinates me. Now, tell me about these cards."

Persistent bastard.

I shook off the thrall he had me under, cocking my head as I said, "I hate you."

"I'm fine with that."

I huffed, really pissed that I'd fallen for his game. Wanting so badly to keep moving that I allowed him to win. This time. "It's how I see the future—or rather, futures. There's a deck of cards in my head, and they flip, showing me different clips of futures depending on hundreds of variables. I make my decisions based on the future I want the most to happen."

He nodded, taking the first step to begin our journey again. "That sounds…boring."

"Boring?" I followed after him, step-clickstepping faster than before as I basically had to chase him. "My gift is not boring."

"No, but living your life based on already knowing exactly what is to happen sounds boring."

"They weren't as powerful in life. I mean, I saw them, but there were times when the pictures didn't make sense. They grew stronger once I died." I brought a hand under my cardigan, pressing my fingers against the spot where my red thread lay. "Besides, it's easier to deal with the bad stuff if I know it's coming."

He glanced over, watching me. Staring at where my hand rested over the tattered remains of my soul connection.

"Do you miss him?"

The change in subject caught me off guard. "Miss whom?"

He nodded toward my hand. "The man who was on the other end of that thread. Do you miss him?"

I yanked my cardigan closed, shaking my head and giving an almost sarcastic laugh. "No, I don't miss him. I barely knew him when I died."

He stayed quiet, watching me, an expectant sort of energy floating between us. Wanting more but staying silent as a way of controlling me. I didn't like it, but I had allowed us to go down this path. I needed to finish the journey.

Finally, I sighed. "The connection was broken by his decisions and the Fates when I was quite young, long before I'd ever even met him. He danced with death and won, but this was the price." I waved a hand over my chest. "I ended up meeting him—and his new mate—right before I died."

"How did you die?"

"Werewolf. I jumped in front of the man I was to be mated to so he didn't have to be the one to take the fatal blow."

"Why would you do that?"

Too many questions, but at that point, the memories I usually kept locked away had escaped my mental barricades. They played out before my eyes, moments that had been so terrifying at the time now dulled with age and distance. The exhaustion from forcing so many options, from sitting for hours watching the cards flip as I rolled through even the most mundane of choices. Did I have dinner on Tuesday or skip it? Did I walk through the hallway or cut across the sitting room? If I forgot to say hello to my sister's mate, would it start a collapse of the plans I had begun to lay and needed to stay firm?

Because, you see, that moment—my death—had nothing to do with the choices made during the actual battle I had been fighting in. The end of my life had been set long before that. The decisions made years before I had ever even considered walking onto that field to fight with my family had led directly to the moment of that werewolf strike, and everything I'd done in the days leading up to my death had just been locking in the details.

Life played out not in the major milestones but in the smallest of choices, and my choices could not ever be set in stone.

I sighed, my mind cluttered. My memories painful. "I died to make sure my sisters had happy and full lives."

"I don't understand how one ties to the other."

"Which is why I rely on the cards—everything is connected, every action causing a ripple effect elsewhere. Giving the man who was no longer tied to me a third chance at life meant my sisters could live theirs, so I sacrificed myself."

"For your sisters."

"And the man who once resided at the end of this braid, yes." I turned toward him, eyeing his profile. That strong chin and chiseled nose, the cheekbones that seemed rocklike. The harshness in his expression. "What about you?"

"What about me?"

"You said you lived, that you were somehow interacting with women. Did you ever have a soul mate?"

"No."

Flat answer. One that only piqued my curiosity more. "But back when—"

"Stop." His pace quickened, his eyes locked on the horizon. "Stop talking about such things. It is impossible to have a soul mate when you have no soul, and mine's been gone for more lifetimes than I can count. Now come, witch. We need to find a place to camp for the night."

CHAPTER EIGHT

THE NIGHT

The dead slept…sort of.

Nothing we did as the dead seemed as full as when we had been alive, so we didn't curl up in a bed and dream for hours on end. We definitely rested, though. Especially in the Summerlands, where a deep understanding of the earth meant our downtime was more for the land itself than for us. Even the grass needed a few hours of quiet.

I had a feeling the realm of the dead had different priorities.

Still, I followed Grim to a clearing in the woods that felt a bit contained, grayed-out tree trunks and dark boughs overhead closing us off from the rest of the world. Once he had walked the perimeter and decided this would be our resting place, I picked my spot and dropped to the forest floor. My body ached and my mind spun, so there was no long preamble to my respite, no care routine or nightly rituals. I tucked my rucksack under my head in an attempt to create a pillow, pulled my cardigan around me so it became my blanket, and I lay down. Ready to rest.

Grim settled in across from me, giving me plenty of my own space. "Anything else you need?"

I stared right at him, my brow furrowing as I frowned. "Are you my servant now?"

He snorted and turned away, a smirk dancing on his lips. "Hardly. But making your rest time more comfortable seemed the right thing to do."

"Then how about a fire? It's a little chilly—"

"No fires," he said, his voice hard and his eyes like knives when he turned them my way. "We burn nothing here."

I didn't have an answer to that, only more questions that I had a feeling he wouldn't answer, so I pulled my cardigan a little tighter and turned away from him. Trying to escape that stabby gaze.

But as my body began to feel heavier and pull me into a lull, thoughts of being alone in the woods filled my brain. Fear started as a tickle along my spine then grew to something cold and twisty inside me. I couldn't ignore it, couldn't get past it. Couldn't even think of resting when so much could go wrong. When there was always the possibility that I could be left alone…exposed and helpless.

Well, as helpless as an elemental witch could be.

Still, I whipped my head around and caught Grim's surprised eyes, staring right at him as I asked, "You're not leaving, right?"

He cocked his head, his expression blank. "I have no plans to leave you, little witch."

That sounded almost more ominous and less reassuring than I had hoped for. Still, I turned over without another word, staring off into the forest with my back to the reaper just a few yards away. Hoping against hope that I didn't end up seeing those wraiths appear through the darkness.

Eventually, the exhaustion overcame me, and right there, in the land of the dead, a place with a reversed reality desaturated to the point of almost nothing, I rested. Closing my eyes and allowing my mind to relax. Allowing my body to sink into the ground and drowse as the darkness surrounded me. Pressing in a little more with every passing minute. Inching closer and—

I woke with a start, my hand closing around the obsidian amulet around my neck on instinct and immediately focusing on the pale stars shining through inky blackness above me. I had no idea why I'd awoken so abruptly and completely, but in my experience, being pulled from rest like that was not good. I sought answers in silence, using my senses to determine if I was in danger or not. Staying still just in case something dangerous lay hidden in the trees.

I saw nothing but stars, felt nothing but anxiety racing through me, and I heard nothing at all.

Nothing. At. All.

That in and of itself seemed dangerous.

Absolutely no sounds reached my ears, and an intense sense of stillness blanketed the area. The quiet carried weight with it, bringing a feeling of dread to the darkness of the night. Of anticipation. I should have been relaxed and drowsy, should have been ready to close my eyes and go back to a resting state, but that seemed an impossible task. There was no reason for me to be awake, yet something had caused me to shift from deep sleep to alert. Something had smothered the sounds of a forest in the dead of night. I had no idea what that might have been, but it couldn't be good.

I sat up slowly, my eyes trained on the woods before me, a particularly dark pocket drawing all my attention. Seeing nothing but darkness and deeper darkness. The cards in my head silent and still…useless. My cardigan fell into my lap, and my amulet slid softly into place, the metal once again resting against my breastbone. A reminder that I had protections about me. Within me. A soft, cold breeze blew across my bare arms like a message from the Goddess, a gesture of support from my elemental power. The air, I could control, and the strength in that would not abandon me. That breeze came in like a kiss from the mother energies, one that only deepened my sense of worry. Reminders meant I needed to be reminded.

Tearing my eyes from the pocket of darkness, already knowing what I would find, I glanced across the little patch of land where we'd chosen to bed down. I found nothing. No sign of life, no Grim, not a thing left behind. He'd broken our pact on our very first evening together, leaving me alone in the forest. My instincts had been correct, though that realization didn't bring me comfort. I couldn't tell if the tightness in my chest had grown more from the disappointment at discovering Grim's abandonment or anger for the same, but my feelings toward him had definitely veered into the negative realm.

Why make a deal to help me then leave me defenseless on the very first night?

"Never trust the dead," I whispered to myself, fighting the desire to cry in what could only be frustration. But the reaper would not see my tears, did not deserve to know how much his abandonment bothered me. I would control my emotions.

I sat up a little straighter, listening harder as I looked around, seeking whatever had disturbed me. Allowing myself a moment to simply feel the world around me. A stronger breeze blew across the tops of the trees, rustling the branches and needles, causing them to sing a warning song. Yes, the Goddess was trying to tell me something. That I was in danger. That I needed to be prepared. For what, I had no idea, but I would be an idiot if I did not heed her warning.

Without thought, I reached into the rucksack and pulled out the first thing I touched. A small bottle, maybe three inches long and an inch in diameter, with a cork lid covered in wax. Inside sat a sprig of rosemary, a golden-yellow stone, a piece of silver wire, and what looked like salt. A protection jar, if the tiger's-eye that practically glowed in the dullness of the realm of the dead meant anything. I ran a finger over the mark on my wrist, infusing the rune with my energy, before tugging at the fabric band for added power. Clutching the little jar as the stone clinked inside the glass. Relying on the protections from my ancestors instead of the promise of the reaper.

A sudden sound like a wailing sort of scream sliced through the still night air, causing me to jump and cling harder to the jar. I knew that scream, had experienced it a few times already. The danger I had sensed had arrived. The cards in my head exploded into life, flipping and sliding across my eyes, the air moving them forward and back as they showed me what they could of the next few minutes. There was a lot of darkness, though. A lot of unknown events and very little clarity of what led to them. One thing I sensed for sure, however, was that I should not be alone.

"Grim," I called, quietly at first. Stupidly hoping he had remained nearby to keep watch or something. I received no answer, though, so I rose to my feet, took a deep breath, and tried again. Louder that time. "Grim!"

The woods went silent again, scarily so. No breeze, no rustle of leaves, no noise whatsoever outside of my own quick breaths. The band around my wrist grew warmer, the warning clear. The Goddess filled me with a sense of urgency, a need to run, which wasn't likely to happen on my throbbing ankle in the dark.

"This is bad," I whispered, reaching for my walking stick so I could at least try to stay on my feet. "This is so very bad."

With a sudden screech from behind me and a whirling dervish of a shadow enveloping me, it got so much worse.

The force of the wraith slamming into me knocked me off my feet. I twisted as I fell, landing on my back, my walking stick giving me a little clearance so she couldn't lie right on top of me. Her gauzy black robe covered me, almost wrapping itself around me like a sentient blanket. The fabric felt oddly weighted, as if helping her to hold me down. As if keeping me in place as she gnashed those white teeth at me. The memory of that oily black substance burning a hole in the concrete had me screaming and fighting back, but the weight of the gauze restricted my movements. I could barely raise my arms to hold her off, could hardly lift my legs to attempt to unseat her.

Trouble had found me, the serious, life-and-death kind, and I had no plan for how to get out of it. No idea how to escape with whatever was left of the life I had been living. No clue what to do so I could continue on my trek and save my little sister.

Scarlett needs me.

As the image of my sister filled my mind, the protection jar rolled into my arm. I grasped it, witchy instincts surging inside me. Power and intentions and pure magick flowing through my blood. The band on my wrist felt like a circle of fire burning my skin, and the amulet practically glowed in the darkness under the gauzy robe. I only needed one more thing.

"No," I screamed, arching my back and trying to keep the wraith from getting close enough to bite. Clinging to the protection jar as I dug deep into my internal powers. "By the power of the Goddess, I call to the element of air. Release your fury, save your chosen witch."

The wind picked up quickly, howling through the trees. The wraith screamed and turned, no longer showing me her white teeth. Her movement allowed more wind to slip between us, blowing the gauzy fabric off my body. The second the shroud no longer touched me, I could move again, so I reached beside me and grabbed my rucksack, swinging it hard at the side of her head. The bag made contact, spell bottles clinking and the wraith screeching loud and long before diving in closer.

She grabbed on to my walking stick, her grip causing frost to form. Causing the wood to grow unbearably cold. I screamed at the burn of the freeze, not wanting to let go but fearing I'd lose my hands if I didn't. She took the decision away from me, though, when the sister yanked the stick toward her and dove for me again, the rucksack resting on my chest the only thing keeping her from making complete contact. It didn't stop her altogether, though. She pushed against me, thrashing her head back and forth as she screeched, one bony hand grabbing my forearm before zeroing in on my exposed flesh. The rune burnt into my flesh glowed in the darkness, lighting up her horrible face. Making me recoil even more as she tugged my arm closer to her.

And then she grinned, those horrible teeth practically oozing the thick, oily substance from before. My scream could likely have been heard all the way in the Summerlands as the creature bit down, injecting my arm with something that felt like ice and heat and pain all at once. The band around my wrist burned, the jar vibrating in my other hand, but my powers didn't grow stronger. In fact, they ebbed, leaving me feeling tired and weak. Exhausted. The weight of the shroud too heavy to escape from.

My heart broke and my tears fell as I realized I was not going to be able to escape.

I'm so sorry, Scarlett.

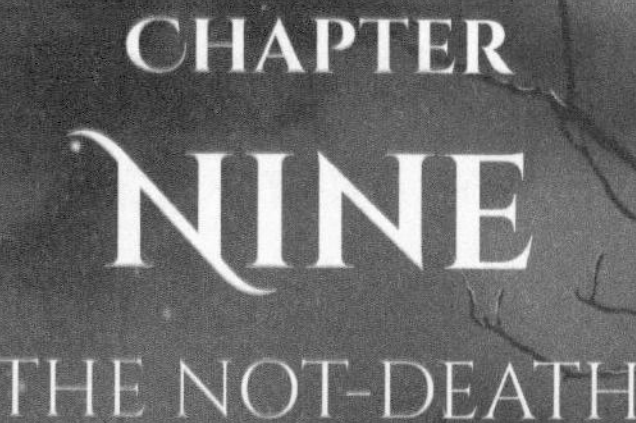

CHAPTER NINE

THE NOT-DEATH

Something funny happened on the way to my second death. Funny as in odd, not funny as in laughing aloud. Or maybe not funny at all because, on the way to my second death, I didn't die.

As my arm burned and tears ran down my face, the wraith suddenly moaned and pulled back, disappearing into the darkness without another attack. The departure left me stunned and shaken, lying on the earth with my walking stick at my fingertips and my bad arm resting across the rucksack on my chest, burning and yet oddly numb at the same time. I had this moment of quiet in the land of the dead—where the darkness deepened to envelop me in a cocoon of velvety blackness and my cold, dull surroundings pressed in. The entire realm smothering me right there. I had this moment of an almost peaceful acceptance of what I knew would be my final ending.

But it wasn't the end that came for me that night.

Grim appeared where the wraith had been as if he'd been waiting for the moment, filling what had been pure darkness with skin so gray it almost glowed and looking down at me with a worried frown blurring his chiseled face. The reaper brought a sense of peace with him, of safety. I suddenly felt protected even though I was anything but. He had left me there alone, ignoring our agreement and my concerns. And yet…I had never been so happy to see another person, even though that person was the Grim Reaper.

I tried to say something, to ask him questions or somehow mumble how I was okay—though I felt far from okay—but my voice wouldn't come. My tongue felt too thick to move freely, and my muscles clenched too tight to make words happen. Locked in silence, I did the only thing I could. I reached for him.

Grim didn't speak either—didn't ask what had happened or if I was okay. He simply stared at my proffered hand for a solid five seconds then lifted me into his arms and ran, moving quickly through the trees. Carrying me away from that place. The world began to spin too much for me to keep my eyes open, so I closed them and laid my head against his shoulder, sinking into the chill of his body. Surrendering to him in that moment, even though, deep down, something close to rage simmered in my gut that would eventually be aimed directly at him. Not yet, though. First, I needed to escape the beasts that wanted to devour my soul.

"Grim," I finally whispered, fighting hard to control the muscles that made words and as my brain filled with a fog unlike anything I had ever experienced. "Something's wrong."

“I know, little witch. Just hang on.” He ran a long way before finally coming to a large creek lined with beautiful if ghostly white trees. He didn’t stop on the banks—he waded right in with me still against his chest, and then he dropped down. He submerged us both. The sudden lack of sound and overwhelming sense of cold shocked me, the cards in my head flipping automatically as the almost ridiculous notion that I could drown slammed into me. I couldn’t see the faces of the cards, though. Couldn’t see enough details to know the future because of an almost impenetrable blur that seemed to be between me and them.

Before I could shift into a full panic at the vision in my head, I was being lifted out of the water. Grim brought me back above the surface then headed for the bank, ignoring the way I tried to smack at him.

“What are you doing?” I gasped, still fighting. Still feeling the odd icy burn of the bite. Still unsure why my cards were so blurry. It was all too much.

Grim didn't answer. Instead, he set me down on the bank—gently and with a care that belied his size and demeanor—and tugged at my injured arm. He stared at the bite for a long time, examining it. Almost growling as he inspected the damage.

"Are you okay?" he finally asked, his voice rough but soft. Angry, for sure, but I had a feeling that was not meant to be aimed at me.

Oh, but I was angry at him. "Where were you?"

"Trying to keep what just happened from happening."

So off trying to keep the Keres sister away from me, without waking me to tell me she was in the woods with us. Stupid man. "Well, you failed."

"I'm aware, witch."

"I have a name, you know."

"I do know, but you haven't invited me to use it, so you will remain the little witch."

"Yeah, well, after all this, I may not ever let you call me Amber."

"As you wish." He looked up at me, his hand tight on my arm. "You were very brave back there."

"I didn't feel brave." I clenched my hand into a fist, wincing as a cold sort of pain spread beneath my skin. "Why weren't you there?"

"I told you—"

"You told me nothing. Why?"

Grim stared at me, his eyes the dark black that always seemed far past death to me. Sharklike. Predator.

"I was trying to convince one of the Keres sisters to control the other, but I obviously misjudged how tempting you are to them."

"So, this is my fault?"

He growled, shaking his head slowly before pinning me with a furious gaze. "I have apologized, witch. The fault has been acknowledged and my failures laid bare. What more do you want?"

I had no answer for him because I just didn't know. So, instead of continuing down a path that might only lead to more animosity between us, I shifted subjects.

"Will there be long-term consequences from her biting me?"

Grim sat silent for a long moment, the pause one that brought fear to my gut. His eyes locked on the bite mark.

"No."

Something in the tone of his voice pinged my instincts. He had just lied to me, but I didn't call him on it. Didn't risk alienating him more—I needed him to help me get to Scarlett, which meant keeping the peace. At least until he proved to me that peace wasn't possible between us.

The cards suddenly flipped inside my head again, the faces blurry and a fog floating around them. I felt my mouth tighten up as I tried to focus, as I tried to see the future the way I always had. As I looked for hints of what was going to happen to me in the coming days.

I saw nothing clearly.

"What's wrong?" Grim asked, still holding my arm. Connecting us.

I shook my head and pulled my arm from his hold, completely off-balance mentally. The power of the air element had always been my foundation. The sight gifted to me by my ancestors the skill that kept me safe. It had grown stronger during my time in the Summerlands, but I had relied on it throughout my entire life and afterlife. I had a sudden sense of being disconnected from air and sight, which left me nothing to ground myself with. Left me no balance in the universe. Something the magick in me despised.

"Witch—"

"Nothing." I looked up at him, keeping my face firm. My mask expressionless. "There's nothing wrong."

Whether Grim believed my lie or not, he never said. Instead, he gave me a single head nod then rose to his feet, holding out a hand to assist me up. "Then it's time to go back to camp so you can rest."

"Won't she come back?"

"No."

"How can you be sure?"

"Because I'll set her on fire if she does."

"You said you burn nothing here."

"And that's why."

My mind spun, options and opportunities lining up. "She can burn?"

He glanced down at me, his face expressionless. The deep night making his dark eyes almost skull-like and hollow. "Everything can burn, especially things that are dead and hollow, like us."

There was a threat in those words, one I couldn't process right then, for I was cold and shaky, suddenly terrified of the wraith coming back. My entire body broke out into shivers, and I stumbled more than once on the trek through the dark woods. Thankfully, Grim held on to my arm and assisted me back to where I had been sleeping. To the makeshift pallet I'd set up with my rucksack as a pillow and my cardigan to cover me.

It wouldn't be enough to ward off the chills racing through my body.

"Just lie down and try to rest," Grim said once he set me down in my spot.

I choked out a laugh. "That won't be possible."

"You need to." He moved across the campsite, settling in against a tree across the way, looking beastly and mean even from so far away. I lay in my spot, shivering, wishing for more blankets. Wanting so much to be warm in that moment. My mind wandering to the juxtaposition in the image of a warm fire in a world devoid of color and heat. How would it live? How would it breathe? *Everything can burn,* Grim had said, including the not-quite-dead wood around us, apparently.

"You need to rest," Grim said, disturbing my mental gymnastics.

"I won't be able to sleep."

"You have to. The morning will bring a long and difficult journey. You need this quiet time to heal."

My body began to tremble once more, and I nearly broke down crying, the fear of the wraith returning, of the blurriness of the cards in my head, of not knowing the future, setting in hard.

I couldn't not ask the one question I almost didn't want to know the answer to. "Are you going to leave me again?"

Grim sat silent and still, watching me. Not answering. When he finally opened my mouth, it wasn't to answer my question at all.

"You don't trust me."

I nearly choked on my laugh. "You have not proven yourself trustworthy."

He nodded once then rose to his feet, walking straight at me. With a sigh and a rumble, he dropped down beside me and settled in against a tree. Reaching, tugging me across the grass, he dragged me over until he had me in whatever spot he had decided I should be in, then patted his thick thigh.

"Lay your head here."

That seemed a little too intimate, though. "Why?"

He grabbed my arm and tugged until I did lie down, until I was lying with my head on his thigh, my eyes focused on the ground just beyond his feet.

"Now I can't leave without waking you up. Rest. I'll make sure you see the morning light."

And though I didn't want to, I believed him. At least for the moment.

"I wish you were warm," I mumbled in a tired and half-sleepy sort of daze, tugging my cardigan around me even tighter as I did as I'd been told. I set my head on his thigh, face pointed outward for some sense of decency, and settled in to rest.

"Me too, little witch. Me too."

And then there was darkness.

CHAPTER TEN
THE MOMENT

The oddest experience of my life might have been waking up on Grim's thigh. Especially considering I had flipped over in my sleep, ending up with my face practically in his lap. I might have been dead, but I wasn't *that* dead. The moment I opened my eyes and realized what exactly I was looking at, I was in motion…away from him.

"Something scare you, witch?"

Grim's chipper little quip and his smirk did nothing to make me feel better.

"Scare me? No. Make me worry about creepy crawlies? Possibly." I turned my back to him, centered and firm, whispering words to the element of air. Focusing on a mundane task to keep from doing or saying something stupid. I worked a simple—but really useful—cleansing spell on myself and my clothes, not bothering to regulate my voice or try to hide my intentions. When I finished, I turned again to find Grim watching me with a hard stare. "What?"

"Why do you do that?"

"Do what?"

"Ask the air to…purify you."

I shrugged and went with the most honest of answers. "I don't want to smell bad."

"We're dead. We don't perspire or deal with bacteria anymore."

I stared at a tree behind him, cataloguing every flaw in the bark. Suddenly uncomfortable with this conversation even though I knew I had no reason to be. "Yeah, well—old habits die hard."

"As do witches, apparently." He rose to his feet and was moving before I could fire anything back at him, which suited me just fine. We needed to begin the day's journey. I focused inward on the cards to see what might lie ahead, but a dark mist still floated about inside my mind. A shadowy blurriness to the visual. I could see cards but not the way I was used to, without the clarity I had built up over the years both in the Summerlands and back home.

Back when I was alive.

I shook off the uneasiness that thought—that reminder of my deadness—gave me and followed Grim to the road, walking stick helping me along the way. Unfortunately, my stick arm was the same one the Keres sister had bitten, and I felt an odd sort of weariness in the bicep. Almost as if I'd done a lot of chores the day before, lifted a lot of heavy things. In truth, I had fought off some sort of demon. Perhaps simple muscle fatigue should have been expected.

The tingling that kept happening in my fingers couldn't be as easily explained, though.

"What's wrong?"

Grim's rough voice pulled me from my thoughts. I followed his gaze to the fingers in question, the ones I had been running my thumbs over to wake them up.

I tugged my hand up into the sleeve of my cardigan. "Nothing."

"Doesn't look like nothing. Are you okay?"

"I'm fine." I looked over his shoulder at the road laid out before us, the seemingly endless strip of half-deconstructed concrete cutting through the trees. "Looks like a lot of flat and nothing."

Grim grunted, continuing to walk ahead and thankfully taking his eyes off me. "That's pretty much what it is. Even in the realm of the living, this is a more rural area. We'll hit a few small cities along the way, though."

"But no cars or people."

He huffed a laugh. "This is the land between. No one should be here."

I took a good look around as I followed him, the crumbling structures and flattened mile markers signs of life. The deep slits in the concrete and massive chunks jutting up toward the sky, signs of death. No one should be there sounded accurate, and yet…

"You are." I cocked my head when he turned to steel me in place with a questioning expression. "Here. You said no one should be here, but you are. The Keres sisters are. That shadow man is."

Grim grunted and kept walking. "There are reasons for that."

"I'm here."

He stumbled slightly, the smallest of hitches in his step before saying, "Again, reasons."

"You know my reasons for being here. Tell me yours."

"No."

I didn't like the finality of that word, nor did I enjoy the way he basically had his back to me. Ignoring me. I'd grown up in a houseful of witches with two sisters, all fighting for attention. I was very good at getting people to stop ignoring me.

"What's your favorite color?"

Grim turned slightly, his brow furrowing as he looked at me in confusion. "My what?"

"Color. Your favorite—what is it?"

"There is no color here."

I laughed, not stopping until he turned around, then ran a hand up and down in the air in front of me. As if I were some sort of prize in a televised game show. "In case you hadn't noticed, I am in full color."

He followed my hand, absorbing the sight of me from the top of my head to my shoes, those dark eyes burning with blue fire.

"Yes, you are." He stalked closer, his long, thick legs eating up the ground between us. When he stood close enough to make me rethink this particular game, he picked up a lock of my hair between his fingertips and ran his thumb over it. "What color is this?"

I blinked, far more nervous at his proximity than I would have imagined. "Brunette. Dark brown, I guess I should say, but my hair color is brunette."

He grunted and nodded once before spinning on his heel and walking off. "Then brunette dark brown is my favorite color."

Something inside me zinged, a warmth I had not expected. I blinked and took a moment to bury whatever I had just felt for the man, grateful for the physical space between us. For a few seconds to remember where I was and what I had been doing before those deep blue eyes had basically devoured me. It wasn't just Grim's eyes, though. It was everything. My entire nervous system had gone a little haywire when he'd moved close to me. When he'd shared physical space with me again. The man had a way of distracting me, that was for sure.

My fingers on my bitten side went numb, tingling a bit, and I rubbed my thumb against them as I followed Grim across the concrete. Thinking. Contemplating.

Ready to get to know that demon a little better. Starting with…

“Are you a demon?”

He didn’t even bother to turn around. “No.”

“Then what are you?”

“I am a reaper.”

“So, that’s not just a clever name, it’s a job title? Is Grim your real name?”

“Yes and no.”

Well, that made no sense. “Yes and no? Grim is and isn’t your real name.”

“No. You asked two questions, so I gave two answers. Yes, Reaper is a job title. And no, Grim is not my real name.”

“Do you remember your real name?”

He huffed a very irritated sigh. “What are you doing, witch?”

"Getting to know you, death thing."

"I am not a death thing."

"Then what are you?"

"I am Grim. As in, a reaper. A demigod of death. You know this already."

I hadn't known the demigod part at all—I had assumed he was some sort of demon. I found interest in that nugget. "Fine. Do you remember where you're from, *Grim-not-Grim*?"

He shook his head, still walking. "Not really."

"That's not a no."

"I've been here too long. I don't even know if my home still exists."

"I could tell you—"

"Ask me something else."

I loved an invitation, even if it was one that closed a door or two. Obviously, things about home and his possible past in the living realm—because he had to have one, right?—were off-limits. But there was always something to learn about someone else. Always ways to break through their little privacy wards and figure them out.

I could have asked a million questions, but I started with, "Cat or dog?"

"To eat?"

"By the Goddess, no. To pet and snuggle or have as a familiar."

"Never had a pet or a familiar."

"But if you could?"

He pointed up toward the sky. "What are those things that fly with the big wings?"

"Eagles? Hawks?"

"Like the one on your bag. They have really big eyes and come out at night."

"Owls," I whispered, the irony of a death demigod liking what we saw as an omen of death not at all lost on this witch. "You mean owls."

"Yes. One of those. I remember seeing one once, and the flying looked very freeing."

"But you fly, don't you? I could have sworn I saw you fly when you were fighting with one of the wraiths."

He shook his head. "Not really. I break apart and come back together in other places, but actual flying—being way up in the sky and aware of your motion and surroundings—is not in my abilities."

"Huh. Okay, so an owl." Again, omen of death. Fascinating. "Good choice, actually."

He grunted his acceptance of that. "What about you?"

"Typical witch—I like the kitty cats." I tiptoed around a deep crevice, gripping my walking stick. My ankle definitely still hurt, but the pain was manageable. Even the deep, uncomfortable throb in my arm wasn't that bad. I focused inward again to try for a visual on my cards, but the blurriness remained. My body appeared to be healing, but my mind had yet to catch up. Disappointing, for sure.

"Next question." I pretended to ponder for a moment, pursing my lips as I hummed, to give him a sense of security. Then I went for it. "Why do you say you have no soul?"

"That's not the sort of question I was expecting."

"Probably not, but I like to keep you on your toes."

Grim looked down, frowning. "On my—"

"It's an expression. Talk about your soul."

His sigh could have been heard all the way in the land of the living. "I was chosen for this role upon my death. To keep me here, Death took most of my soul." He held out a hand to help me around a pit in the concrete, not making eye contact the entire time. "Leaving me with only a sliver keeps me here, unable to fully cross into the afterlife I had coming to me. Unable to return to the land of the living."

"You're stuck," I murmured, a sinking feeling hitting me. The torture of being trapped in a realm you didn't belong to, of being denied your rightful afterlife, seemed horrific. Grim could have been some sort of mage or druid, could have been fated for an afterlife leading to reincarnation like us witches. The could-haves piled up in my brain, but I wouldn't say them—I didn't need to add to whatever negative feelings he had about his reaper duties. "That sounds awful."

"I am accustomed, little witch. And I take on projects now and again to remind me of the living." He turned to gaze at me, looking me up and down in far more of a suggestive manner than I was prepared for. "Like you."

"I'm not a project."

He shrugged. "Says you."

It was my turn to sigh. "Fine. Easier question this time. Beach or mountains?"

We continued on that way for what I assumed was about an hour—one of us asking a question of the other, both answering, and me trying to focus on the cards so I could see what was coming. At one point, the blurriness got so bad that my head began to ache and I had to pause.

Had to stop walking and grip my skull as if I could somehow squeeze the pain away.

"What is wrong, witch?" Grim's fingertips felt warmer than I expected as he grabbed my arm, his hold far more gentle than normal.

I shook my aching head. "The cards are fuzzy, and they're giving me a headache."

"Your future cards?"

"Yes."

"So, stop looking at them. We can make our own future."

I huffed a laugh, letting go of my head and hoping the rest of the pain would dissipate quickly. "I don't do anything without consulting the cards first."

"That sounds confining."

"Maybe in your world, but it's very comforting in mine." I walked past him, head up but aching, walking stick in full step-clickstep use. Fingers and ankle burning. I had a sudden thought that the cards certainly hadn't helped keep me from being injured so much already, but I pushed that down. That was the sort of thought that would get a witch stripped of the gifts provided her—especially one who should be thankful she was alive in a weird, undead sort of way. Being ungrateful was not appreciated by the Goddess.

We walked the rest of the day, often in silence, occasionally bickering back and forth. There was no attack from the Keres sisters along the way, no threat to deal with. Just large boulders of concrete to find ways around and deep pits to avoid. Still, by the time the sun appeared to be setting and we were headed for a copse of trees to rest for the night, I was absolutely exhausted. My head, arm, ankle, and fingers all hurt, but so did my back. In fact, my entire body felt as if I'd been beaten up, which I sort of had. In a way.

"Here," Grim said, pointing to a spot in a small clearing. "You should bed down here. I'll take a look around to make sure we're safe."

But I wasn't paying attention to him, because in the distance, just past the next line of tress, I saw water. What looked like fresh water. Lots of it.

“Is there anything in there that might eat me?” I nodded in the direction of what had to be a lake when he turned to look at me. “I feel like bathing.”

“We don’t sweat.”

“But we do get achy after days on an injured ankle and after an attack like last night. Will I die if I get in that water?”

“You’re already dead, but nothing bad should happen to you if you go for a swim. It will be cold, though.”

“I’m okay with cold. Be back in a bit.” With that, I limped my way across the forest to the waterline. I started by just taking off my boots and cardigan, stepping into the water with my skirt hiked up to my thighs. Grim had been right—the water was cold. Very cold, and yet it felt so refreshing. I continued farther out into the lake, enjoying the feel of the sandy bottom between my toes. When the water rose to my knees, I yanked my skirt and top over my head and tossed them to the shore. My simple tank top came next, a habit I held on to from my living days. One habit I had stopped once I'd ended up in the Summerlands had been wearing underwear, so there were none of those to worry about. But layering under my shirts with a tank top? That would never end.

Naked and more than a little cold, I walked deeper into the lake. The water felt amazing on my sore muscles, even my ankle no longer protesting my being on my feet. But this was water, which meant I didn't need to be on my feet at all. I pushed off the bottom to float, lying on the top of the water and staring up at the darkening sky as I let my own buoyancy keep me from drowning. Taking a moment to be at peace in this strange world. The cards flipped, the blurriness and fog still bothering me, but I ignored that aspect and simply gave thanks to the universe for the gifts I continued to receive.

One card popped to the forefront, clearer than the rest. A picture of Grim on a lakeshore, staring off into the distance. A lakeshore that looked awfully familiar. I turned my head slowly, not at all surprised to find the man watching me. Without shame, I dropped my feet and regained my footing, the water not quite covering my breasts. Naked and at least partially exposed.

Grim didn't look away.

"Is there a reason you're here?" I asked, raising my voice to be heard across the distance.

That heavy brow furrowed, an expression close to anger flashing across his face. "I have prepared a resting spot for you."

"Fine. I'm coming out."

I had expected the man to turn around, to give me a modicum of privacy as I exited my lake bath. Apparently, I had expected too much. Grim not only didn't turn around, he didn't stop staring at me as I walked closer, making no effort to hide the fact that he was practically devouring the view of my naked body. Witches were not brought up with the puritanical shame of the non-magickal people around them, so I had no qualms or fears about being undressed in front of Grim. His stare—the intensity of it—brought out the goose bumps in me, though.

I made it all the way back to shore, to the clothes I had tossed carelessly from the lake, before addressing him. "If you were a gentleman, you wouldn't be watching me."

He grunted, looking me up and down again with obvious interest. "If I were a gentleman, you wouldn't be here with me."

I rolled my eyes and opened my mouth to reply, but Grim reaching for me stopped the words in my throat. He didn't touch my skin, though. Instead, he grabbed the skirt from my hands and took it, shaking it out before holding it up for me to step into. He then tugged it up my legs, settling it on my hips. Next came the tank top, also shaken out and held out for me to slip easily into. My shirt, too. The man stood there, my clothes in his hands, dressing me. Such an intimate act. So caring and almost subservient. Such a moment of pure confusion on my part as I allowed him access to this private part of me that I should have been hiding.

Once he placed the cardigan around my shoulders, he sighed. “It’s a shame to cover up such lovely artwork.”

If I’d had a working heart, it likely would have been beating loud enough for him to hear. My entire body had gone stiff, frozen in place under that dark stare, even as my soft and squishy insides turned to some sort of burning hot jelly. The man had a gift for making me feel things I didn’t want or need to feel, and this time, that feeling was need. Desire. Want.

Grim had just made me feel *aroused* for the first time since before my death. A fact I had been solely unprepared for.

I clutched my cardigan to my chest, taking a long, hard look at the man before me. The demigod. The reaper Grim and yet not. The cards flipped through my vision but remained too blurry to focus on, my mind too smoky to see through. I was on my own. No cards, no peeks at my future, no way to know the right or wrong response to such a perfect flirtation with the most imperfect man.

“Thank you,” I said, refusing to back down and yet definitely not ready to grow whatever had just happened. I, instead, chose to turn away from the man who had rattled my body and my brain, walking back to the campsite without another word spoken.

But I was definitely no longer cold from the lake.

CHAPTER ELEVEN

THE SHIFT

"Are we going to make it to St. Ignace today?"

Grim grunted, leading the way out of the woods and back to the road of horrors. The sun peeked through the clouds a little more than usual, making this dreary, grayed-out world far brighter than I was used to. There was still no real color to see—just shades of gray, shadowy in places and less so in others—except for me. Though my rust-colored cardigan and patterned skirt looked a little duller than usual. Or perhaps I had been adjusting to the grayness of this world.

Either way, the drabness of everything was downright depressing and did nothing to make me feel awake or energized. In fact, the dreariness almost seemed to sap my energy.

"Do you ever miss colors?"

Grim turned, grabbing my hand and helping me up the embankment to the concrete. My ankle still hurt even though it remained wrapped and I used my walking stick, but I wasn't about to tell him that. He must have known anyway, though, because he stared at my injured ankle for a long moment once we made it to solid ground.

"How is your ankle?"

The man grew more predictable with every hour spent together. "It twinges when I put weight on it, but it's bearable."

He grunted, reaching for me. Gripping my arm tightly as he turned it over to see the remnants of the bite mark. My cardigan sleeve covered the worst of it, but he saw enough. Saw the black and ugly. The dark lines spidering down my forearm.

"And this?"

"I'm fine." I yanked my arm away, moving past him. Step-clickstepping my way north. "So…St. Ignace. Do you think it's possible?"

"Perhaps." Grim appeared beside me, matching my pace as he looked straight ahead. "Depends on how well you keep up with me."

"I'll keep up."

"We're slower because of your injuries."

"I said I'll keep up. Don't stop because of me."

"How's your arm…really?"

I huffed, struggling to see the cards for the right answer. My chest tightening as the blur blocked my view. The faces were still unclear, the fog too thick to see beyond. Ridiculous.

"Grim—"

"Witch." He looked my way, face hard. Eyes stabbing me in place. "I don't like disobedience. Tell me how your arm is really doing."

"You're a jerk," I said, but then I sighed and shrugged a single shoulder. Refusing to look at him again. "It burns and my fingertips tingle a lot, which is uncomfortable, but it's fine."

Grim grunted—a signature sound, I was learning—and continued on, also staring straight ahead again. Silent for a long time. Long enough for me to assume the subject had been closed. Long enough for me to be even more irritated when he proved me wrong.

"Your definition of fine lacks truth."

The wind picked up as my temper flared, blowing across the stretch of highway and causing little funnels of dust to rise. Grim watched one such funnel as he continued walking, looking almost impressed. His expression warmed me from the inside for some reason. I was not interested in worrying about that particular detail, though.

"My definition of fine is *fine*. Not good, not perfect, not on death's doorstep. Something I can deal with and allows me to continue moving forward through the day."

"You already came through the door."

It took me a solid three seconds to allow those words to ping-pong through my head before I uttered a very articulate, "Huh?"

"You said, not on Death's doorstep. You already came through the door. And you're already dead. You are not *on* Death's doorstep but through it."

I sighed big and loud and overanimated because I had no patience for him at that moment. "Not death as in *you*. Death as in a concept—as in the end of living. As in—" I struggled to find more words that could explain my meaning, but they wouldn't come and I didn't like the growing tightness in my chest, so I scoffed and finished with, "It's just an expression."

"Like your *fine*. Not in the least bit true but something to say."

My temper snapped, the breeze blowing harder and stirring up more dust. I kept walking even as Grim stopped, even as branches and debris flew past me. The magick of the air element had never really been as flamboyant as some of the others.

Azurine—my sister with an impressive control of the water element—could make a tsunami form in a pond. Scarlett—fire witch—could set herself and just about anything else on fire and give entire communities a show of flame and smoke. Me? I controlled the air, played with fire, and had a decent understanding of earth magick. My powers were never quite as showy as the others, but tornadoes and earthquakes didn't need to be showy.

Grim seemed to pick up on my powers pretty quickly. "Witch. Stop it."

I bit back my grin, still walking away from him. Still building the power of the wind around us. I couldn't see the cards well enough to watch this play out, but I could sense them flipping. Could see flashes of gray and black, of white and ashy cream. I was about to play again, to increase the speed of the wind or have it start to spin around me, when a flash of bright orange passed by my vision on a card. Too quick to understand what it was, too blurry to grasp context and place. But it was orange, and it was floating in the air, not lying across a floor.

"Scarlett." My word came out on a whispered breath as I froze, the wind dying down immediately.

"Witch?"

"My sister…I saw…" I took off at a faster clip, the step-clickstep brighter and steadier. "I saw her. This is the right decision. I have to get there."

Grim grabbed my arm, yanking me to a stop. "And we will, but rushing over this minefield is dangerous and can lead to more damage of your body."

"My body is fine."

His lips twitched, a slight smirk rising. "Not good, not perfect, not on Death's doorstep."

I hated that he quoted me so correctly. "Yes. Exactly that."

"Then I reiterate my opinion—your definition of fine is lacking truth." He leaned in, growling deep in his chest, still holding my arm with his big, rough hands. "Your body is far more than just fine."

If I had been breathing, my breath would have caught. As it was, my entire body felt practically paralyzed for a split second by the meaning behind those words. The context. The double entendre.

Grim released the full power of that smirk then grabbed my arm again, tugging me with him as he continued on his way. As if he hadn't just crossed a line into some sort of strange new territory with me.

As if he hadn't just made my entire focus shift from Grim, the scary, mean Death god, to Grim…

The man who saw me as more than just fine.

CHAPTER TWELVE

THE TUNNEL

The afternoon plodded on as time spent on the road to Hell, Hades, or whatever terrifying place roads of broken concrete and pits of despair led to seemed to do. Grim—always quiet—grew even more so as we walked farther north. For good reason. The road grew rougher and more treacherous with every hour, becoming difficult to traverse at times. There were moments when Grim would stop and grunt before grabbing my arm and directing me all the way to the embankment. There were moments when I would wobble along a tiny path of concrete over a trench and have to yell for him to offer me a hand. He always did, never leaving me alone to deal with the possibility of falling. Of maybe dying. Would I die again if I fell in there? Or would I simply be trapped in an eternity of nothingness down a deep hole?

"Shut up, Amber," I said to myself, shaking my head. Grim shot me a look that screamed questions, so I shrugged. "Just thinking thoughts that are not worth worrying about or entertaining. How much longer until St. Ignace?"

He pointed eastward, where, off in the distance, I could see a sliver of what looked like a broad, white swath between the darker gray foreground and the horizon.

"We're close."

I blinked, staring harder at that swath of white. "Where are we?"

"We're in Mackinaw City, the last town in the lower peninsula before the bridge."

I nearly squealed in excitement. "So, we're almost—"

"No." He huffed, staring off at the same cold- and icy-looking site I was. "We still need to make it across the straits to St. Ignace, then over to the island. We'll likely need to cross the ice bridge."

"It's not cold, though."

"This is—what do you call it?—the realm of the reversed. That waterway is always either icy enough to tempt fools to cross it or with waves large enough to swallow the ferries that people take over in the realm of the living. There is no in-between."

Ice sheets that could break apart at any point or waves. Big waves that could drown us. Could we even drown? Grim seemed...well, grim, so I had to assume there was some sort of possibility of a death beyond the current death we were existing in. Assuming got me into trouble, though.

"Can you die?" I asked, my voice sounding quieter even to my own ears. I looked up when Grim turned, the expression on his face giving nothing away. "Here. In this world. Like in the waves or down one of these pits. Can you die?"

He grabbed my hand, leading me past a particularly jagged section of concrete before answering.

"My existence here can end, yes."

My stomach dropped, my long-dead heart almost jumping in my chest. "Then why are you doing this?"

"Doing what?"

"Helping me."

"Because I choose to."

"But if this is dangerous for you—"

"You are dangerous for me, witch. Yet I choose to spend my time with you." He tugged me closer, looming over me as he yanked me to a stop right against his big body. "I have lived an eternity in Death's realm, leading confused souls to their afterlife or helping to have them—" he cocked his head, those deep blue eyes darkening to more of their black state "—erased from our collective consciousness."

I nodded. "That's a really nice way to say—"

"That I fed their souls to Death himself? Yes, it is. But that's part of my job. And I am very good at my job." He leaned in, seeming to inhale. Almost…sniffing me? "Right now, my job is to get you through this realm and back to your Summerlands."

"You don't want my soul?"

His lips kicked up into a wicked smirk, his head dropping closer. "I want a lot of things from you right now, my little witch, but I can assure you your soul is not on that list. The rest of you…"

There was a promise in his silence, a sense of anticipation I hadn't felt from anyone in so many years. It enveloped me, warming me from the inside, and making my head spin a bit. Grim had laid his cards out right there on the concrete for all the world to see. And I saw them. I knew what he had in his hand.

But I wasn't ready to bet against him.

"So, we hope for ice," I said, rubbing my thumb over my numb fingertips and pulling away, reclaiming my hand and unable to hold his gaze.

We stood in a tense silence for a solid five seconds, likely the longest five seconds of my life or death, before he finally responded.

"Yes."

One word broke the tension. Without another syllable, he turned, following the road once more as if nothing had happened. As if he hadn't just… done *that*. As if the entire world hadn't just shifted under my feet.

Perhaps it hadn't shifted under his.

I drew back into my mind, seeking answers from the cards. Needing their comfort. They flipped and danced, but it was still so hard to see the fronts of them. So difficult to make decisions and see the path my decisions would cause. I felt unmoored without access to my gift, lost in a sea at night with no starlight or moon to guide me to safety. Not since I was a child had I been unable to see the cards flip, unable to at least glimpse the future my decisions created. The loss of that grew bigger and darker with every passing hour, the fear of never seeing in my way again slowly eating me alive from the inside. I couldn't focus on it, though—couldn't give in to the stress and fear. I had a sister to save, a job to do. I had—

The sudden touch of Grim's hand against mine had me jerking back to reality. He lifted my wrist, staring at where my thumb had been running back and forth over the tips of my fingers.

"Still numb?"

I both loved and hated when he spoke in his concerned voice. "Sometimes."

"And the bite?"

I pulled my arm against my chest, not wanting to show him how dark and almost sunken-in the area had become. Not wanting him to see the flesh slowly turning grayer than not. I just needed to get to Mackinac Island, save my sister, then make it back to the Summerlands. The witches there would fix it.

"It's fine."

"We have already established that you operate under a lacking definition of fine."

The need to roll my eyes felt almost unstoppable, but disrespecting the Grim Reaper seemed like a bad plan.

"Let's keep going," I said, tucking my fingers into the sleeve of the cardigan so he couldn't see them and keeping my eyes locked on the tree line in the distance. "I want to get to the island tonight if possible."

He looked northward, eyes scanning the highway. "There's an overpass around the next curve, then we should be able to see the Straits."

"You don't sound confident."

"The road is not to be underestimated."

"Yeah, well…neither am I."

I led the way forward, not even grumbling under my breath when he slipped in beside me as if to guard against the solid concrete beneath my feet. He seemed to feel the need to be extra protective the farther north we walked, something I would not refuse. Protective Grim made things long dead inside my body come back to life, made places I hadn't even thought of grow tingly and warm. The demigod was still quite the jerk, but he cared enough not to want me to fall to my undead death in some concrete prison. Perhaps I'd set the bar a little too low, having spent a couple of decades mostly around dead female family members, but I could live with that. Or be dead with it. Whatever option seemed the most likely considering my current situation.

Please Goddess, turn off the part of my brain making me think such thoughts.

When we made it around the next curve, I finally saw the overpass Grim had spoken of. It stood like a bridge over the freeway, big and dark and made of more concrete with steel supports on the edges. Pretty much exactly what one would expect a freeway overpass to be…

If that overpass led to Dante's seventh circle of Hell.

"We have to go through *that*?" I pointed at the darkest of dark tunnels I had ever seen. The space under the bridge oozed malevolent energy, the danger practically lighting up like a beacon from the top. *Come in, my child*, it sang. *Come inside. You'll be safe here*. Which I knew was a total lie. "This is crazy."

Grim stayed silent for a long moment, staring at that shadowy space beneath the bridge. His brow furrowed in thought or, more likely, worry. Perhaps anxiety. Probably coming close to downright fear.

"To go around it would take hours."

I stood strong, my head up, eyeing the black hole before me. Refusing to give in to the fear the space instilled in me. Refusing to back down. *For Scarlett*. "Then we go through it."

"The trek may be dangerous."

"And the rest of the trip has been safety central?" I grabbed *his* hand this time, pulling him with me. "Come on, demigod. Let's get this over with."

But my exterior bravado did not match my interior fear. That tunnel looked like a direct path to someplace I did not want to go, someplace that could take me to an end worse than the one I was already existing in. That tunnel looked like the sort of place I would get lost in, losing my access to the Summerlands—and, therefore, my family—forever. But I had to go through it. Scarlett lived on the other side. Saving her was my goal.

If I'd had access to my cards, I would have looked to see if taking the longer trek around the tunnel would have paid off with her still being alive once I reached her, but I had no foresight. No way to know if the gamble would pay off. So, through the tunnel we would go.

I could only hope we made it out the other side.

"Stay close," Grim murmured as we approached the entrance, the mouth of the overpass yawning wide and leading into pitch blackness. "The road above is only three lanes, so it's not a very wide overpass."

"Then why can't we see the other side?"

"Good question."

With no answer. We crept into the tunnel, Grim leading the way and holding tight to my hand, keeping me right up against his big body. Three steps in and the world went dark—darker than I had expected. I stuttered to a stop, just a quick pause, but it was enough for Grim to look my way. To turn his head in my direction. Something I should not have been able to see in the inky blackness. But I did, which ended up being a problem.

Grim's eyes caught mine and speared me into place, the light coming in from behind me just enough to bring my nightmares to life. Like those of some sort of nocturnal animal hunting its prey, they glowed in the darkness. Not white or yellow or green, though. Of course not. The Grim Reaper had eyes that glowed bright red. Big, absorbing, and deeply terrifying orbs pointed right at me.

The light from outside the tunnel might have seemed to be absorbed by the darkness, but enough got through to give me a moment. To allow me to see his face. Just barely enough to make out the shape and shadows that created him. The man who had wrapped my ankle, carried me away from danger, and dragged me up a few embankments. The one who thought my body was more than fine.

That chiseled face frowned as he watched me try to regain my mental balance. I'd already seen his eyes change colors—from black to deep blue—so why this new color shocked and scared me so much, I had no idea. But I needed to get over it.

"It's okay," I said with a nod. "I'm fine."

He huffed—likely because he didn't agree with my use of the word fine—and turned back to the north, continuing into the tunnel. I gripped his hand tighter and kept moving, following him. Mirroring his movements when he took his next step. If I had been brought up in another faith, another circle of beliefs, I would have thought I was being led through Hell by the devil himself. But witches didn't believe in devils or Hell, so the analogy didn't quite fit.

We were about thirty steps in when a loud crack sounded from above us. Grim jerked us to a stop, his glowing eyes shooting upward as he yanked me forward. I slammed into his big body, my hand still caught in his, my other resting on the muscles of his chest. His growl reverberated against me and around the space, low and deep with a threatening sort of rumble. Something I could see and feel through our touch. Something that grew louder and stronger…until I realized he wasn't growling at all.

A sound like the world was about to tear itself apart grew from both above and below. The earth—usually so solid underneath me—began to shimmy in a way I had nothing to do with. As if preparing herself to open wide. As if ready to cave in below my feet. I swallowed hard, trembling. Clinging to the reaper as if he were a lifeline. A way through. An escape route.

At least until he began to pull away from me.

"Grim?"

"Hush." He crept two steps forward, dragging me with him. Putting space between us but holding tight to my hand while trying to progress through the darkness. He moved us slowly, one step at a time, deeper into the nothingness.

The trembling within me grew stronger, my entire body quaking as the sounds from above and below increased. Shaking so hard, Grim stopped to look down at me with those glowing, demon eyes.

"Witch? Are you—"

He never finished his question. One second, I was focused on the tremor running throughout my body, and the next, that movement shifted, dug deeper. It became something close to a tremor from below, and then it became what felt like an actual earthquake. A massive crack sounded, the noise exploding in the dark, making me yelp and jump as I tried to turn to focus on the direction it came from. The sound reverberated, though, and I ended up spinning in a circle with no sense of where the danger would be coming from. I lost contact with Grim for just a moment, a mere second, and I took one step in what I thought was the right direction. Where I expected land to be below my feet, there was nothing, and suddenly, I was falling.

Time slowed, my descent into the belly of the reversed earth taking much longer than I would have expected. I could almost see the land I should have been on, could almost spot the deeper shadows that would have been Grim's shoes turning slowly in my direction. *Too late*, I thought to myself. *Far too late*. I had made a mistake and would pay the price for it, living out the nightmare of what would happen if one of the crevices along the road swallowed me whole. Leaving Scarlett to die her early death alone and without her sister to guide her to the Summerlands. I would spend my eternity in a seam of the earth, I was sure of it.

Sure…until a cold, rough hand grabbed me by my outstretched hand and pulled. I flew forward, screaming as my hair was gripped and yanked and pulled upward as well. Nearly falling over when my feet hit solid ground once more.

Grim's evil eyes flashed my way, that demonic red visible even in the pitch-black tunnel, before he grabbed me. Snatched me right off my feet and into his thick arms instead. Before he picked me up off the ground and started running with me. Within seconds, my back hit something hard and solid as what sounded like a total collapse of the bridge around us began. He pressed me into the solidness of what I had to assume was a wall and covered me with his body, the entire world seeming to explode behind him. Shielding me from the worst of it.

Almost making me forget that I was the one with the powers in this place.

"Boreas, child of Aeolus, keeper of the north wind, hear my call!" I screamed, gripping Grim's shoulder tightly as I sank deep into the magick within me. "Protect your air witch in her time of need."

I raised my arms, relying solely on Grim to keep me from falling, and drew three sigils in the air. One for strength, one for protection, and one for fighting. I blew the three shapes into the atmosphere, chanting spells in my head. Releasing my magick into the universe to feed the other air gods and goddesses. A strong wind blew through the tunnel, coming from the north entrance, toppling what sounded like boulders and making Grim grunt and push me harder into the wall to stay vertical. The air moving against the tunnel walls created noise so loud I nearly had to cover my ears, the sound reminding me of heavy freight trains screaming along the tracks by the coven house I'd grown up in. Crushing in their volume and constant thunderous rumble.

I buried my head in Grim's shoulder and hung on, letting Boreas fight whatever energy lived in the tunnel. The sounds went on for what felt like minutes, the earth shaking all around me for far too long as the wind pounded through. Grim stayed steady through it all, though. Solid and sure and protective as he pressed his body into mine. And when it ended, when the quiet of the Reversed reigned once more and the air went still, he kept holding me. Kept me safe. Kept protecting me with his own form.

A big, strong body pressed in every way against my own.

My arms had somehow become wrapped around his neck, my legs around his waist, with my ankles crossed behind his back. We were one tangled mass of beings, both shaking way too hard. Both sort of coming back online from absolute terror to…something else. Light penetrated the tunnel for the first time, allowing me to see the man holding me up. The one keeping me secure to his own detriment. The one who pulled back and stared down at me with a look of pure fear on his usually stoic face.

"Witch?"

Out of pure habit, I focused inward, wishing and hoping to see my cards. To know what was coming. But there was still nothing, and I finally cracked under the weight of not being able to rely on my gift.

"I still can't see my cards." I clutched him tighter as tears of stress and release and likely a little adrenaline crash began to track down my cheeks. "I'm so used to making all my decisions based on what they show me that I don't know what to do."

Grim ran a finger over my forehead, those glowing eyes locked on mine. That red lighting up the harshest of angles on his face. "The cards—that so-called gift—hold you back. Don't seek validation from a future that can be destroyed with the smallest of decisions. Do what you want…right now."

So, I did.

I leaned forward and pressed my lips to his, needing some sort of physical comfort after three days of fear and attack and body-breaking exhaustion. Needing to feel something close to normal in that moment when a second, soul-crushing death had been so close. I kissed him because I needed to feel a connection to another person.

I kissed him because I wanted to be kissed.

Thankfully, Grim kissed me back. Deep, body-arching kisses that turned my cold skin warm and had me scratching at his shoulders in an attempt to bring him closer. The rock wall stood hard and rough against my back, the dust in the air falling and coating our skin, but it didn't matter. Nothing mattered. Grim's body was against mine, rocking into me, soothing an ache I hadn't even recognized had needed soothing as he slipped his tongue into my mouth to tangle with mine. Time stopped, everything outside of that tunnel disappearing. There was no danger, no need to move, no quest to complete—there was only him and me and the feel of his lips against mine, the vibration of that rumble I'd heard from him before quivering against me, and the total connection of my body to his. A complete surrender on my part. And his.

The crashing of rocks falling from overhead to the ground right beside us broke us apart, Grim's growl growing deeper as his glowing eyes took in the new threat before returning to watch me. I struggled to keep from pulling away, noticing for the first time how my fingers had gone ice-cold and the bite mark on my arm actually throbbed. My injuries moving into the forefront of my mind. Magic moment between us broken and reality restored.

I needed more light to see what was happening, and we needed to get the heck out from underneath the collapsing concrete bridge.

"We should move," I whispered, dropping my legs from around Grim's waist to the floor. He grunted, his growl constant, his hands going to my hips as if to hold me in place.

"I thought we were moving."

“I mean out of this hellish tunnel.”

He nuzzled into my neck, tugging me into his arms as he murmured, “Does that mean I can move into your hellish tunnel?”

It took a solid five seconds for his words to register, and when they did, I had to laugh. I also had to reach up and run my fingers along those sharp cheekbones. To feel the thick scars against my skin. It was something I could no longer resist. Grim’s growl turned lower and deeper with my touch, sounding more like a purr than I’d ever heard from him before. I nearly kissed him again at the sound of it. Had an urge to sigh when he grabbed me by my hips and tugged me closer, bent my body to fit his, and purred into my neck. The man did not disappoint.

“Answer me, little witch,” he said, words rumbling against my skin.

But some questions needed evading. “That was a horrible pun.”

Grim laughed against me, wrapping his arms around my waist and pulling me into a tight embrace. One that soothed a lot of fears inside me for reasons I was not yet prepared to contemplate.

He set me down carefully, sounding almost regretful when he whispered, “Time to go.”

I nodded, finding my feet once more. “Ready.”

He pushed me away and grabbed my hand, tugging me along after him through the darkness once more. The bridge continued to crumble, the falling boulders dangerously close and terrifying. I put my faith in Grim to get us through to the other side, but even faith needed a little help sometimes, so I whispered spells of protection along the way. Murmuring the words I’d been taught as a child to help me through scary or dangerous situations.

“One, two, three, nothing harms me. Four, five, six, no mean tricks. Seven, eight, nine, all is fine. Count to ten. Everything is Zen.”

Whether it was Grim’s absolute determination for us to reach the end or my spells—or a combination of both—we finally made it through the shadowy abyss of the tunnel and out to the other side. The low light shining from the sky hurt my eyes for just a moment, and I squinted to compensate. It took me about half a minute to be able to truly look, to see, to take in the sight.

And when I did, I gasped and gripped Grim's hand like the lifeline it had become.

What lay before me was both absolutely gorgeous and completely terrifying.

The Mackinac Bridge—the longest suspension bridge in the western hemisphere—lay broken and crumbling across the strait. Suspension cables snapped and entire sections of concrete just…missing. There was no way across to St. Ignace. No easy path to the Upper Peninsula or across the strait to Mackinac Island. There was nothing but massive waves and a feeling of absolute and utter malice coming from the water.

"What now?" I asked, clinging to Grim as I tried again to see the cards. To find a solution. I got nothing in return, for once having no plan and no way to decide the right course of action. I was floating in a sea of indecision.

Grim, on the other hand, did not even hesitate. He grunted, looking over the landscape ahead of us just as I did. Likely noticing the same details—the island in the distance, the hard, solid ice over the waterway, the Upper Peninsula anchoring the other side of the Mighty Mac. I could practically feel the energy of my sister from where I stood, and yet I had no direct way to get to her. I had to make it to that island, but how?

As if he'd read my mind, Grim said five words that chilled me to the very tips of my soul.

"We take to the ice."

"What ice?"

He nodded toward the waves. "Tomorrow, there will be ice. For now, we rest."

"But it's right there—"

"And impossible to reach." He loomed over me, creeping closer. Bringing our bodies together once more. "I need you to trust me, little witch. Tonight, we rest. Tomorrow, we head to Mackinac."

But trust was hard-won, and one steamy kiss after a moment of terror was not a foundation to build it on. I stared out across the water, sensing the threat from the waves crashing against the rocky shore. There was definitely no way across now. If Grim said there would be ice tomorrow—as impossible as that seemed—I would have to put faith in his words. At least a little. This was his world, his domain. He would know what to expect.

I hoped.

"Fine," I said, uncomfortable but somehow knowing this was the right thing to do. "We rest now."

No kissing, I told myself. *No fraternizing with the demigod.*

I had one night to get through. One more stretch of extra darkness to survive.

Then tomorrow, I would see my sister again. Hopefully.

CHAPTER

THIRTEEN

THE SURRENDER

With the darkening of the night in the reverse world came tension. Not from fear of some creature coming to steal my soul or something creeping out of the shadows—though those thoughts actually did bring a little stress to the party. But no, the main source of pressure came directly from the energy between Grim and me. After the time in the tunnel—after basically dry humping me against the wall—he'd gone silent. His energy almost angry. I had no idea how to deal with an angry Grim. Though honestly, if Grim had only just turned angry and scary, what had he been the rest of our walk north? Or rather, what was he now, seeing as he'd been angry and scary the entire way?

Grim had become…terrifying.

"I'm going to loop around the site, make sure we're alone."

I glanced up at the sound of his voice, completely on edge. Even his tone for such a simple statement seemed cutting. I could no longer tell if this tension emanated from him…or from me.

"Checking for the shadow man?" Because I hadn't forgotten him. Or the wraiths.

"That man is the last thing you need to worry about here," Grim said before rising to his feet. "Stay here while I check the forests."

"For danger. Not shadow man danger, but… something. Right." I tugged my cardigan closer around me, trembling slightly. The terror of the tunnel had left me feeling a little off, a little shaky and cold. Something I was struggling to get past.

Grim stepped closer, looming over me with a glare on his face that sent ice down my spine. “The most dangerous thing in these woods is me, little witch. Remember that.”

I held his gaze, fighting my own body not to show how shaken I felt. Grinding my teeth before saying, “In the woods…but not in the tunnel.”

His face fell, something close to surprise showing in those dark eyes. I almost reached out for him, almost rose to my feet so I could wrap my body around his once more. So I could crawl into the comfort of his hold on me and forget where I was for just a few moments.

But that wasn’t a possibility.

“Witch—”

“Go. Patrol.” I raised my arm, giving him a mock salute. “The witch will stay put.”

He huffed, looking ready to begin an argument, but then turned in what I could only assume to be retreat. He headed into the woods without another word, disappearing into shadows as if he wasn’t the least bit afraid of them. And maybe he wasn't—maybe he had become so used to this reversed world that there was a level of comfort in the consistency of its danger. He believed he was the most dangerous thing in this area, so maybe he truly wasn't afraid of the deepest of shadows. Or maybe…

"How long have you been here?" I asked the second he appeared from the shadows once more.

Grim sent me a deep frown. "What do you mean?"

"Here. In this realm between true death and the living. How long have you been here?"

He settled onto one knee, brushing aside twigs and dry leaves. Clearing the area at my feet for no good reason that I could see. "I do not remember."

"What was your time on the living plane like?"

"I have no—"

"What was it like?"

He huffed, dropping heavily into a spot before me. He grabbed some of the smaller pieces of wood and began stripping them of their bark, his eyes locked on the mindless task. I thought for a long moment that he simply wasn't going to answer. But that moment passed.

"I was a fisherman, I know that. The village I lived in was on a big, beautiful sea."

"You don't know which one?"

He shook his head. "I have been here too long to hold on to those memories, but I see flashes of myself on the water. Fish. Nets."

He stacked some smaller branches in a vertical cone shape, adding dead leaves and things beneath it. I recognized the shape but said nothing, almost afraid to be hopeful.

"I think that's how I died," he said, still focusing on building what appeared to be a log pile for a fire. "In the sea."

He grabbed a couple of stones from the ground and began clicking them together, obviously trying to create a spark to start an ember. Hope bloomed.

“Are you making a fire?”

He grunted, not looking at me. Focusing awfully hard on the rocks in his hands. “You seem cold.”

“You told me no fires.”

“I am making an exception.”

Something warmed inside me, a feeling like a soft glow of some sort. This man—this demigod of death—was building a fire for me. Something to keep me warm and comfortable. The sweetness of the act did not go unnoticed, nor did the fact that Grim had no idea how to start the fire. I didn’t want to interrupt his fight with the rocks, but I could do better than that.

“Here,” I said, crawling right next to him. Settling with my knees touching his. “Let me help.”

I concentrated on the little pile of leaves at the base of the cone, focused on the gift they were about to give me. On the sacrifice of the wood about to be consumed so I could stay warm.

When I had the energy built, when I was sure I could accomplish what I needed, I reached forward, set my hand against the leaves, and said, "By the Goddess, vibrant and bright. Give me a spark to conquer the night."

Grim huffed when nothing happened, which only made me grin. I looked him square in the eye, smiling at his disbelieving expression, and I snapped my fingers. The fire made a whooshing sound, flames dancing up the cone of wood faster than either of us probably expected. Grim actually fell backward in his effort to move away from the fire. Me, I stayed close. Watched it grow for a minute. Watched it devour the wood we had fed it. I sat and absorbed the energy of life from the flames, letting my soul be revitalized.

"Thank you," I whispered, keeping my eyes closed as warmth grew around me. "This has been missed."

"How did you do that?" Grim asked, sounding absolutely flabbergasted.

I shrugged, opening my eyes to stare into the flames. "I'm a witch."

"You can make fire? Just like that?"

"Sometimes. It's not my preferred element, so it can be hard to control, but I can burn things."

"Have you ever lost control of it?"

I laughed, memories of my life with my sisters flooding me. "More than a few times. I once set a porch on fire."

"Did you get in trouble?"

"No. My sister—Scarlett—is a fire witch. Everyone assumed she did it, and I let them believe it."

Grim settled in next to me, his body touching mine. Both of us watching the fire. "That sounds devious, little witch. I wouldn't have thought you would do such a thing."

"Neither did anyone else in the coven—that's how I got away with it."

He moved closer, pressing one hand into the dirt at my side. Practically leaning over me as he steeled me into place with those deep blue eyes. "You're a naughty one."

The air changed on a dime, grew heavier and harder to breathe. Memories of those moments in the tunnel—of the switch from terrified to turned on—flitted through my mind. My lips tingled as if Grim were already kissing me again, and my hands ached with the need to touch him. Feel him. Pull him toward me.

Thankfully, I didn't have to.

"C'mere, witch," he said before tugging me into his lap. He stared down at me with those intense eyes, his cheekbones and jaw so harsh in the firelight. Hands running up and down my back, he pulled and shifted and yanked me exactly where he wanted me to be. "Feel that?"

I nodded, knowing what he meant. The hard ridge sitting between us. The thick, hot pressure of him so stiff making my body clench and weep. There were so many other things to be doing, so much to worry about. But this moment, this brief second of time, was so very needed. A dalliance in the middle of an emergency. A few selfish minutes of pure pleasure.

I was all in on being selfish, but first…

“Why did you start a fire?”

Grim grunted, staring back at me. His face so intense. “You needed it.”

“You seemed almost afraid of fire a couple of days ago.”

“Not afraid—I hate it. Fire can rage in this realm, and I don’t like to be around when it does. But you needed it.” He grabbed my hand, pulling my trembling fingers to his face to kiss the tips. “You haven’t stopped shaking since the tunnel.”

“Grim—”

“Are you going to keep talking, or can I start pleasuring you now?”

I shut my mouth with a click, simply staring as he groaned and tugged me in close. Not refusing. Not even thinking of refusing. Almost happy to surrender. Finally.

Our coupling started simply enough—Grim leaned in for a deep, plunging kiss that sent my body bowing and all thoughts of fear and loss and pain scattering. There was nothing but Grim and me and the newness of us together. His hands—so big and rough and strong—ran all over my body, owning me, demanding my flesh give way to their needs. To their desires. I was nothing more than prey, mewing and rocking and wanting so badly to please the predator before me so he would keep me safe. So he would protect me. And—to be frank—so he could get me off with his beautiful depravity.

“Lie back, witch. I want to touch you,” he said, his voice a low rumble in the night. I did as I was told, pivoting at my hips to lean against his knees. He tugged up my skirt, not quite exposing me, and his hand disappeared underneath. “I’ve been watching you gallivant around for so long. It’s about time I get my hands on you.”

I gasped at the first contact, rolling forward slightly. Unsure if I wanted to move into the feeling or away from it. Grim didn’t give me the option.

“Are you okay?” he asked, almost like a gentleman. There was nothing gentlemanly about the way his fingers glided over my precious flesh, though.

"I'm fine."

He grunted, his irritation at that word plain. "Witch."

A word, a name, and a command—all in one. I had no answer for him, so I pulled him to me instead. Spread my legs a little wider. Gave him more room to touch and feel. I consented with my entire body.

Grim sighed, those dark eyes staring down at me. Glinting in the firelight.

"I'm not a gentle man."

My lips kicked up in a smile that I couldn't have stopped if I tried. Had he been reading my mind or were we simply that connected in the moment? It didn't matter. This time, I knew the answer he needed.

"I don't expect you to be."

I had no more words for him. Not once his fingers delved deep inside my flesh. Not once he took control of my body with one hand. Within seconds, he had me rocking over him, my eyes closed as sensations I had almost forgotten about flooded my body. It had been so long since someone had touched me like Grim did, so long since I had felt that climb toward a physical release. And while his hands on me felt amazing, it wasn't enough.

"More," I whispered, the power behind my word bringing up a small wind across the clearing. "I need more."

"How much more?"

I sat back up, leaning in for a kiss as I tugged Grim's hand from between my legs. As our lips pressed together and our tongues tangled, I reached between us to unfasten his pants. Slipped my hand inside to feel the thick, hard length of him. He growled deep in his chest as I began to stroke him carefully. Softly. Knowing he'd want more. He'd need it.

"Witch—"

"My name is Amber, and I want you inside me. Now."

Grim did not need to be told twice. Without hesitation, he lifted me off his lap and flipped us over, his thick body lying down beside me as I reached for him. Slapping my hands away, he tugged my skirt down and off, then cupped my pussy. Not entering, not focusing on my clit—he simply held on to me as if in ownership. Something I had never realized could feel so good. Something that made me moan and arch.

"By the Goddess, what are you doing?"

"Whatever I want…Amber."

My name on his lips melted something inside me, had me reaching to hold him tighter, bring him closer. Try to absorb him somehow. He pulled my shirt up and leaned in, lapping at my nipple before biting down. I screeched and jerked, the shot of pain only enhancing the pleasure as he kept that hand firmly pressed against me. As he began to move just slightly, barely enough to tease. And yet somehow enough to have me rolling my hips into his hold. Had me clawing at his shoulders and chanting his name. The man had somehow turned me into an animal, and I loved it.

The moment he pulled his hand away from my body, I whimpered, drawing a low, rumbly chuckle from him.

"Easy, little witch. I'll take care of you. I always take care of what's mine." He laid me down, tugging off his shirt and pants before climbing on top of me. Him almost naked and me…not.

"Take this off," I said, trying to tug my shirt over my head. Grim shook his head, allowing me to raise the shirt far enough to lock my arms into place before lying on top of me. Trapping me in my clothes.

"This will be more fun."

"I can't move."

"I know." He slipped a hand between us, this time moving beyond cupping me to slipping a couple fingers inside. I arched and groaned, shifting my hips in an effort for more. For deeper. Grim held back, though. Almost seeming to test the waters. Teasing me with his touch before removing it.

"Are you going to be a good witch?" he asked, removing his fingers and bringing them to his mouth to lick. "Or am I going to have to punish you?"

By the Goddess…

"What if I say that depends?"

He growled like a beast, coming to lie atop me. Spreading my legs with his hips. "Punishment, it is."

Without warning, Grim lunged forward, sliding inside me and filling me deep. I squealed and tried to kick myself away from him, but he let his weight pin me into place as he began to thrust in and pull out of me. Every push brought a shot of pain, every retreat brought a longing for more. There was no way to separate the two, no way to focus on anything other than the sensations Grim brought out of me. Well, that and his dirty mouth.

"Fuck, you're so damn soft. And hot. How are you so hot? I've never felt something so warm around my cock." He adjusted his position, raising up on one arm and stroking slower, deeper. More intense as he drew out the sensations he caused me. "I've waited so long for this. I wanted you naked in that field of flowers with that blue sky overhead, but I'll take you here in this hell. I'll take you however I can get you."

Words were too hard, my brain focusing solely on the pleasure building within me. Still, something pinged inside me, a thought about what he'd said. Something that needed to be discussed. But talking was overrated, especially when every muscle felt tensed and ready. Anticipating the upcoming fall.

"Grim," I groaned, clenching around him. Gripping him tight. "I need more."

"I've got you." He drove into me, hard and fast and still somehow pressing on my clit. Making me shake and moan and lose what little control I had.

"I want to feel you come, my little witch," he said with a grunt and a position adjustment that had me keening. "I need it."

"So, make me."

And he did. With growls and bites and deep thrusts and pinches that set my body shaking. I came more than once, collapsed and practically fell asleep a time or two along the way, only to be woken up by Grim again teasing my flesh and making me feel things I never had before. And when we were finally done, when the fire had died and Grim lay beside me in the quiet night, I began to laugh.

"That's not the response I was expecting," Grim said, sounding far unhappier than I'd intended him to be.

"I'm sorry," I said, clutching at the arm he had thrown over my body. "I'm thinking about how ridiculous it is that two dead people just had sex in the land of the undead while traveling to save a living person from an adversary we know nothing about."

Grim grunted, tugging me close. "Sounds impossible."

That ping from earlier went off in my head again, his words coming back to me. "As impossible as us being together in the Summerlands."

He sighed and tugged me closer, holding on as if afraid I might pull away. "Yes, impossible."

"You watched me."

"I did."

"That's why I kept seeing the door."

"I had no idea you could see it—you shouldn't have been able to."

"Well, I did. I felt you watching me."

He leaned in, dropping his face into the crook of my neck. Biting me for good measure before speaking against my skin. "I watched...and I coveted. I wanted you from the first moment I saw you."

Something in his tone made me pull away, had me turning in his arms to face him straight on. Had me staring at him with a wary sort of excitement boiling within me.

“You watched me die, didn’t you?”

His nod was his only answer, his eyes locked on mine as the silence built.

I shook my head, trying to determine how I felt about that. “You saw Aoife come direct me to the Summerlands.”

“I did. The necromancer is known in these parts, but I was still surprised to see her with a witch.” He dropped his gaze, unable to hold my stare as he murmured, “I would have helped you cross over. I wouldn’t have let you stay here.”

“Oh.” Which was all I could say, all I could think for the moment. Grim had been there when I died—watched me struggle in this very land before being led to the Summerlands. He saw me. He—

“Stop thinking so hard, little witch.” Grim wrapped me back up in his arms, practically covering me with his body. “What’s done is done. I’ll get you through this and back to where you belong.”

With a sigh that did nothing to help relieve my trepidation, I snuggled into his hold, his words reverberating in my head. My gift of precognition was gone, my body damaged, my injuries worsening. I had no idea if we would make it to the island, no clue if we even had a chance to be on time. All I could do, all I could put my faith in, was my will to save my sister.

And Grim.

CHAPTER FOURTEEN

THE BRIDGE

Grim had been right—the next morning, the strait between the peninsulas, as well as the lakes to the east and west, lay covered by a solid mass of ice stretching as far as the eye could see. Thick enough to walk across but unlike any ice I'd ever seen.

"It's weird that the ice isn't cold." I reached out to touch a tall shard, the temperature not even registering as anything other than slightly chilled. "Don't you think it's weird?"

Grim didn't answer; he just grunted and kept walking. Well, he kept pulling me along behind him. The man hadn't let go of my hand since we'd broken camp for the day's walk. Apparently, the Grim Reaper was a bit smitten with me. Not that I minded.

We were underneath the Mackinac Bridge, long referred to in my family as the Mighty Mac. Spanning about five miles long, it had always seemed to me to be such a feat of engineering. It had once been the longest suspension bridge in the world but had been relegated to the longest in the western hemisphere at some point. Title or not, the bridge connecting the Upper and Lower peninsulas of Michigan was awe-inspiring. And I had chosen to walk underneath it.

I would have loved to say that the decision had come with the knowledge that we would cross successfully or that my cards had shown me the way, but that would have been a lie.

As I walked on ice that could swallow me up at any moment, heat filled my bad arm, the bite mark pulsing with pain. Half of my hand had gone numb at some point that morning, and the cards had gotten even harder to see. Something was wrong, but my instincts told me to keep it quiet. Not to complain about it. So long as I saved my sister, whatever was happening to me was worth it. I'd sacrificed before—I could do it again. So instead of complaining, I pulled my good hand from Grim's hold and tried to shake the numbness and the pain away out of the bad one without attracting his attention.

"What's wrong with your hand?" Grim asked. I sighed and stopped shaking it. Attempt to keep him clueless—failed.

"Nothing. Did you know the bridge sways in the wind? One of the elder witches took us to the U.P. a few times, and crossing the bridge was always so scary to me."

"It's a dangerous bridge."

"Two cars have just…blown off."

"Not really." Grim stopped, waiting for me to reach him before holding out a hand to help me across an almost slushy segment of ice. "One flew off, killing a woman, but it wasn't the wind. She was driving too fast and hit the median, which sent her careening across the northbound lanes and over the edge. The other car going over was a suicide."

"Wait…really?"

"Yes." No explanation, no more background or facts. Just…yes. And I believed him.

If someone had told me the ice had disappeared beneath my feet, I couldn't have been more surprised. "How do you know all this?"

"I am not Death, but I am not blind to his ways or the ways of the sisters who have hunted you. Now come, we have another few miles to go before we can leave this ice and prepare for the next trek eastbound."

He caught my eye, a slight glow forming around the iris. Like in the tunnel. Like last night when we…well, when we had been alone. And naked.

And he had your arms secured at your sides so you couldn't move while he filled you.

The heat in my arm spread fast, making me feel almost flushed. If I had been alive, the skin on my neck likely would have given that fact away. Death stole that ability, something I found myself thankful for as I followed Grim across the ice.

We were coming up on the second support towers—about two-thirds of the way across the strait—when something made me pause. A movement that broke the monotonous grayness, a shadow appearing where one hadn't been before and definitely didn't belong. I stared at the huge concrete support standing before me, the one I knew continued under the ice to the bottom of the strait, trying to pinpoint what had captured my attention. What had made me look. And then I saw it. A shadow. Or rather, a shadow man.

"Grim." I pointed when he looked my way, too afraid to say any more words. To be heard.

Grim stared for a moment, his heavy brow drawn tight, before he followed my pointing finger to see the shadow man on the tower base. The way his body went stiff for the briefest of seconds told me more than his words did. Especially when I felt those words were lies.

"It's nothing to be concerned about." He grabbed my hand and tugged me closer to him, walking just a little faster than before. "We need to keep moving."

But moving meant passing the tower, which meant walking right by the shadow man as he watched from above us. A terrifying thought, and one I wasn't looking forward to. But I put my faith in Grim, who refused to let go of my hand. A modicum of security in a moment fraught with fear.

A moment that grew even scarier when the shadow man spoke to us.

"They won't let you do this," the shadow called from directly above us. "They have given you a little space, but they will turn on you, too. Your beloved Margaret can't stop her sister."

Grim tugged me closer, walking faster. Giving me no time to stop and look up. We had made it about three-quarters of the way between the tower and land when he finally slowed down enough for me to tug my hand away.

"Stay close," he demanded, as if there were anywhere for me to go besides where he led me. As if I were dumb enough to go wandering across the ice just because.

My temper made the wind blow a little stronger and colder than before. I couldn't just ignore it. "Who was that, and what did he mean?"

"His name is Hypnos, but he's not important."

Hypnos...so he had a name. "And what did he mean? Who are the *they* he spoke about?"

"I told you—it's nothing."

"It certainly seems like *something*."

"It's not. Let's go—St. Ignace is right there." He continued on his way, practically leaving me behind in his rush. I, meanwhile, kept a steady pace and tried to distinguish the emotions swirling inside me. Attraction to Grim, sure. More because of what had happened—and not been spoken about—the night before, naturally. Fear for Scarlett, definitely. A little fear for myself as well, though that one I kept squashed, and I had a feeling a lot more lay hidden beneath the surface that I wasn't ready to examine. But there was also something solid and cold, something like a wall building. Not between the living and me or the Summerlands and me, but between Grim and me. He knew who Hypnos was, knew exactly what he meant when he yelled about Margaret and her sister. He didn't trust me enough to tell me, though. That stung. It also pissed me off, which caused my witchy side to grow more agitated. The wind howled for a good stretch as I fought to control my temper.

We made it to the land at the base on the north end of the bridge without another incident. Grim helped me up the embankment and onto the roadway leading from the bridge into town, though that word seemed to be a broad and overreaching description for what the place was in the Reversed. No people, no busy businesses or trucks flying past. Just empty streets, broken light posts, and derelict buildings looking abandoned and rotting in place.

"It's scary here." I grabbed Grim's arm, needing something like comfort from him. I remembered too late that Grim didn't really *do* comfort.

"It's scarier on the ice, which is where we're headed. Come."

I hated to be dismissed. The wind whipped past, the tightness in my chest blooming. The words coming practically unbidden.

"Who's Margaret?"

"No one."

A small funnel cloud formed before us, making Grim stop in his tracks. Making him actually take the time to turn and look at me.

I did not give that opportunity away. "Who is Hypnos?"

Grim sighed, looking skyward. "They are not of importance to you. What is important is that we cross the ice to the island where your sister lives. Or is that no longer the priority?"

His words cut, the truth behind them spearing me. This entire trek had been about Scarlett. I needed to remain focused on that.

"Fine. Lead the way."

Grim did just that, reaching for my hand and tugging me along behind him. A quick walk later and we again stood on the shore, looking out across a massive swath of ice. On the horizon, shadowy and seeming so very far away, sat our destination. Mackinac Island. A tourist spot touted for being trapped in time with a no-car policy and only a handful of year-round residents. I'd been a few times as a young girl, spending summer days with my sisters riding bikes around the island, with their famous taffy and fudge to fuel our fun. There was an energy on the island that had fed my sister Azurine's connection to the element of water, that had made her gift grow in leaps and bounds whenever we had spent time there. I'd also enjoyed an increase in my connection to air, standing on top of bluffs and absorbing love from the breezes blowing across the water.

The island had always seemed so magical to me. But standing across the strait and knowing I'd need to cross the dangerous ice bridge to get to it changed my perception. It now appeared dark and forbidding, as dangerous to me as the abandoned town I stood in. I let the cards fly, wishing and praying to every deity I could think of to give me a glimpse—something small but sure about what was to come. I received no such vision. There was just the vague sense of the cards flipping and a rolling fog filling my brain, heavier than ever.

My gift hidden from me.

Grim finally turned to me, looking slightly unsure for the very first time since I met him. "Are you okay to make the last trek tonight? I'd like to continue on since the ice seems solid."

Solid, yes. Dangerous, also yes. But the very thought of the stretch before me being water with waves and undertows seemed so much worse. "How far is it?"

"Seven miles. If we can keep a good pace, it will take us about two hours."

I blew out a long sigh, evaluating the sky. The darkness already hung low in the west, the shadows of dusk beginning to dance across the icy flat before us. In two hours, it would be night for sure. We couldn't fight the sunset forever.

But that didn't quite make sense.

"Why does the sun go down here?"

Grim frowned. "What?"

"We're in the Reversed. Everything is dead and the sky is dark, yet there's a sun that will set and bring darkness with it. Why does the earth continue to spin and make the sun go up and down?"

"It's our memories."

"What is?"

"This." He waved an arm. "All of it—the roads, the town, the sky. It's all a mirage, fake. What we see is based on the memories we have from the same spot in the living plane."

"But then why can't we just…apparate?"

"Do what?"

"Apparate. You know…Harry Potter-like. Move from one location to another without the actual exertion of walking there. If this is nothing but memories, then land and time here are not real. Why must we put in the effort when we should be able to relocate without actually moving?"

Grim grunted and huffed, looking angrier than I'd seen him all day. Looking completely off-balance. "Your words and questions won't make us arrive any faster. Would you rather we start the journey to the island tonight or not?"

The wind blasted between us, blowing his hair and mine. Making us both look as if we were warriors about to go to battle. And in some ways, I guess we were. But the battle was both external and internal. Outside forces and this…whatever it was…between us.

At that moment, Hypnos appeared once more, a dark spot on the horizon. Distant but obviously there and watching. I didn't even bother pointing him out to Grim because I already knew the man would dismiss my concerns, just as he dismissed my questions about navigating our way through this world. My trust in him cracked at that moment, not breaking completely but becoming damaged. Becoming something I no longer could put my faith into blindly.

I had never felt more on my own than in that moment, but I couldn't give up. My sister needed me, which meant I needed to get out on the ice.

"By the Goddess," I whispered before climbing down the embankment and placing my first foot on the ice. A clinking noise came from my rucksack with that first step, a reminder of the supplies my family had given me. I stopped and pulled the bag from my back, digging into it and grabbing the first thing that felt right.

"What is that?" Grim asked, staring down at me with a face pinched by confusion.

I examined the little bottle I'd grabbed, my smile coming unbidden as I noted the care my family had taken to protect me. Pink Himalayan sea salt rested on the bottom, covered by a layer of a dried herb that I could only guess was basil. Witch's salt covered those layers, thick and black and filled with so much power, I could feel the vibration through my fingers. A sprig of rosemary rested on top of that with a few cloves and stones at its base. Black onyx chips glittered on top of all of that, moving the rosemary around as I shook the bottle. A rune had been carved into the wax that sealed the cork topper, the same one that had been carved into my hand. A symbol of protection. The perfect spell in a little jar, just for me.

"Witch," Grim said, stealing my attention away from the magick in my hand. "What is that?"

"A spell. It's protection in a bottle." I tucked the spell jar into my pocket, words of protection whispering through my mind. The rucksack stood open before me, though. Calling to me. My instincts screaming that I wasn't yet done with that bag. I reached inside again, this time pulling out a soft, velvet pouch that held untold treasures. I pulled open the strings of the pouch and reached inside, tears coming to my eyes as my fingers touched the contents. As I figured out exactly how much my ancestral coven had protected me.

"What's that?" Grim asked, moving closer and staring at the pouch. "I feel…death coming from it."

I nodded and pulled out a handful of items—a chicken's foot, a few long, thin bones likely from a bird, the pelvis bone of a rabbit, a coin, a key, a shell, and a pink stone. My eyes burned with unshed tears as I looked over my bounty, my long-dead heart warm and open.

"Osteomancy." I chuckled softly, gripping the bones in a fist. "They're throwing bones. The witches of my family in the Summerlands packed these for me. They must have known I would lose access to my gift, so they gave me another divination tool."

Without waiting for his response, I dropped into a crouch, shook the items in my hand, and focused my thoughts on the trek across the ice. On if we would make it or not. I brought my hand to my face to blow my useless breath across the pieces then tossed them onto the ice before me. They landed in a chaotic sort of beat, the sudden noise fading to nothing once they were still. I dropped to my knees and examined the fall, pulling on all my instincts to understand the message being shown.

“What do they say?” Grim crouched beside me, staring down at what had to look like a random mess before us.

There was no randomness to me.

I picked up the bots and baubles, working my way from the farthest to the closest. Keeping my eyes down so as not to have to look at him. “Danger ahead but we’ll make it.”

He grunted. “Of course we will.”

I ignored the attitude of his statement and kept tucking the items back into the pouch, saving the final three for last. The ones closest to me, which meant the most important message of the throw. Two leg bones crossed over each other right next to the pink stone. Rose quartz—a crystal that signified love and romance. The bones crossed so close to it were sending me a very clear message.

A betrayal was coming. One that involved my heart. That involved Grim.

I finished picking up the bones and dropped everything safely into the pouch, returning it to my rucksack without another word. Centering myself for what I would feel when I looked into the eyes of the man who was soon to lie to me, to deceive me.

But I had to…eventually. "Ready for the ice?"

Grim caught my eye when I looked up, an unreadable expression on his face. Not that he had ever been the most emotive demigod around.

"We should go." He reached for my hand, tugging me after him once more. Leading the way across the ice bridge that had always been dangerous in the living realm. I had no idea how bad it could get in the reversed realm, but it had to be worse. A thought that irritated me. Or rather, focused my irritation on the man holding my hand.

This trek would be dangerous, and Grim refused to share with me how to stay safe other than to cling to him. A fact that rankled something deep and dark and angry under my skin. That unearthed the independence I had once been known for when I'd been alive.

No one ignored a Weaver witch for long.

"Be ready, witch." Grim grabbed my arm, yanking me closer as I slipped through a patch of slush on the ice. "You won't get a second chance out here."

My skin grew warm, my temper fanning flames inside me. I closed my eyes and called on the power of the element of air, receiving no warning. No rush of wind to stop me. Receiving nothing that would cause me to worry. I had been relying on Grim to help me so far, but I was close. And once I made it to the island and found my sister, saving her would be solely on me. I could not allow my feelings for him or the way he stoked my temper to get in my way.

The Goddess would have to be my guide.

Scarlett, I thought. Staring out across the ice. Focusing hard on the island seven miles away. *I'm coming*.

A slight breeze picked up and blew along my cheek, a comforting sort of touch from my most powerful ally. A reminder that my gut instincts were stronger than assumptions or worries or even the cards themselves.

I knew what I needed to do.

"I'm always ready." I took one step forward and pulled away from him, giving myself over to fate. Knowing the Goddess would protect me. Heading straight for Mackinac Island at last. "I need to get to my sister."

CHAPTER FIFTEEN

THE ICE

The ice bridge to Mackinac was a famous phenomenon in the area, particularly among those who liked to snowmobile. During the depth of winter's grip, the island would become isolated and inaccessible due to the ferry being unable to cut through the ice and planes being unable to fly through the weather. The ice bridge offered a path from St. Ignace to Mackinac Island, but the bridge came at a cost. Many people had fallen through over the years, most of them dying in the icy waters. Drowning as their snow machine sank to the depths. The ice could never be underestimated.

"It's downright spooky," I said at one point, crouching down to touch the hard surface over the water. "Why isn't it cold?"

Hypnos—the shadow man Grim had told me not to worry about but who had been following us across the ice—laughed from his spot far to the right of me.

I shot Grim a glare, the wind picking up as it always did when my temper flared.

"What are you not telling me?"

Grim's expression didn't change. "Stop touching the ice. We need to keep moving."

But that just made me want to touch the ice more. Made me want to lie down on it, let my entire body make contact. Made me drop to my knees and spread my arms wide, hands resting on the dry, but not at all cold, surface. "I wonder if the water—"

Grim grabbed me and pulled me to my feet, yanking me along with him until I could stand on my own. Forcing me to move. The jerk.

"I can walk," I said, pulling away from him.

The man refused to let go of my hand, tugging me after him. "Prove it."

The wind practically howled past us, spinning snowflakes high into the air before letting them settle to the hard surface below our feet. My temper had been stoked, my anger flaring under my skin. My air element coming to remind the demigod that he wasn't the only one with skills. Grim turned to catch my eye, face as hard and unreadable as ever. I raised an eyebrow as the wind whipped past him, waiting him out.

Finally, he sighed. "We don't talk about the water when we're on the ice."

"Why not?"

"Because I said so," he replied, his tone one that definitely didn't sit well with me. His words ones meant for a child.

I was no child. "You need to mind how you speak to me. I'm getting sick of you bossing me around."

He grunted, not even bothering to look my way. "And I'm getting sick of you trying to get us killed."

"We're already dead."

"Not dead enough." He stopped, holding out an arm to tug me to a halt alongside him. His dark eyes scanning the horizon. "We'll need to make an arc to the north. There're bubbles to the south."

I couldn't see what he did, but the concern in his voice spoke to some sort of instinct within me. I may have been mad at the man, may have been slowly building a wall between us in my mind, but I wasn't going to ignore him on this. If he said the ice would be more dangerous to the south, we would go north.

We moved along a little slower than before, keeping close to each other, and both of us watching the ice. I had no idea what I was looking for, but I couldn't stop staring at it. Couldn't look away from the odd expanse. Shadows sometimes danced underneath the cloudy surface, making patterns and striations that seemed unnatural. Currents, I told myself. I doubted the lie, but any other options were more terrifying than the man shadowing us. Whatever was under there, I didn't like it and had no intention of exploring to find out more about it. So, I followed Grim, hoping against hope that we would make good time. That we would reach Mackinac Island before dark.

I didn't want to be on the ice in the dark, that much was for sure.

I'd never been so far out on solid ice, and the sensory overload of it only made me want to move faster. Growing up on a small lake, I had seen a water mass frozen over in the winter. I had skated and walked across it a thousand times. Nothing that small cracked and moaned the way the ice bridge did. Nothing sat as open and unprotected, allowing the winds to howl past. The ones that were definitely not being caused by my own tumultuous emotions. Being out on the small lake of my childhood had never given me the heavy sense of doom that looking out across the Strait and realizing we were miles from land with no place to find safety should something go wrong did. The only options were to go back or to keep moving forward, and my sister was forward. I would trek on toward her.

A little over ninety minutes into the walk, when we were finally obviously closer to Mackinac than St. Ignace, we came across a section of ice that had water on top. Grim held his arm out again, his universal sign for stop, the hard lines of his face looking more pronounced than ever as he stared at the liquid. He'd been concerned about bubbles earlier—water on the ice had rendered him nearly immobile.

"Grim?" I grabbed on to his arm, the tenseness of the muscles making my stomach clench and my heartbeat race. "What is it?"

"Let's head south," he said, ignoring my question. "See if we can get past this section without dealing with the water."

"It's only like ten feet of ice that has water on it. What's the big deal?"

"We head south."

Oh, the man made me cranky. I didn't push him further, though. He grabbed me and led the way south, keeping his eyes locked on the small bit of water on top of the ice. Water that should have been solid. It seemed to be under the wet surface, though. Of course, the ice also seemed to be frozen, and yet I felt perfectly comfortable traipsing across it in my skirt and cardigan. The whole "looks cold but not actually cold" still bothered me, still made me wonder why I didn't freeze as I walked on solid ice. A thought that made for a good distraction for only about thirty seconds, because that was when a shadow danced below the ice again, heading straight toward where the water sat on top of the ice. An urge to understand filled me, made me want to follow that shadow. Made me question Grim and his absolute fear of the water. Was the water cold? Why wasn't it frozen? We were less than a foot away from a small patch of it. I could find out. I could answer my own question since he appeared reluctant to give me any information.

I was already crouched down before I realized what I was doing, already reaching with arms seemingly not under my control when Grim screamed from across the ice. The sound of him, the word *witch* cutting through the strange, almost thumping sound coming from underneath me, didn't matter. Nothing did. Just the questions dancing in my head and that shadow enticing me to touch, to feel, to understand the power of the water beneath my feet. I reached forward—

"Witch, stop!"

A sudden wind blew across the ice, bringing Grim's words to my ears and clearing the cobwebs from around my brain. A wind that wouldn't stop blowing, growing like a tempest and making snow dance on its currents. My brain cleared once more, the power of my chosen element pushing aside whatever had led me to almost…

What?

"Grim." I moved as if to rise to my feet, but my shoes slipped on the ice. I wobbled slightly, reaching out to stop my fall. Setting my hand down to find my balance. My fingertips touched the water—warm, so very warm—and the wind immediately stopped. The world growing silent in the span of what should have been a heartbeat.

What had I done?

Grim roared a growl that sounded completely inhuman and raced west as if trying to rush back to St. Ignace, which made no sense. Mackinac was closer, I didn't—

A sound like a gunshot interrupted my watching Grim run, and the ice split under my fingers. I crab walked backward, eventually regaining my feet and jogging backward toward Mackinac. The crack split a section between Grim and me, running in an almost straight north–south line. Separating us.

"Grim!"

He was midstride when the ice beneath him must have given way. He went from a big, dark shadow running on the ice to nothing. Gone. Like a video game or a magic trick, just…disappeared.

"*Grim*!"

I had taken just two steps forward when I saw Hypnos in motion. He flew across the ice exactly like one of the wraiths, practically made of nothing but smoke. Within seconds, he arrived over the spot that Grim had fallen through, splashing water all around as he flattened his smoky form to cover more ground. I watched, terrified, unsure what to do. How to help. What had even happened.

Suddenly, Hypnos flew straight up, a second shadow following him. Perhaps being pulled by him. I couldn't see clearly enough to tell, but the overall smoky form was definitely bigger than before. It swirled and rocked, not at all smooth in its movements anymore. Breaking apart as it reached a pinnacle. Two distinct clouds of smoke circled each other on the way back down in ways that made no sense to me. I couldn't tell what I was seeing, but it looked awful and aggressive, like smoke fighting. Fog battling.

The energy in the air grew hot and mean, the feeling of a confrontation solidifying in my mind. The shapes also began to blink in and out, confirming my suspicion—Grim and Hypnos were fighting. Over what, I had no idea. Who controlled the fight, I had no clue, but they were definitely sparring.

Until they weren't.

The energy shifted within the blink of an eye, calm dropping like a curtain. Forming a void for a few seconds, like before a tornado when there was no energy, no air. Just stifling humidity and pressure. Then that departed, and the world of the reverse felt normal once more. Or, as normal as it could be. The wind began to blow again, caressing my skin like a concerned parent. A sensation I desperately needed in that moment.

Finally, the shadows separated, becoming two distinct forms once more. One flew off, floating along the ice as it made its escape. The other dropped to a spot about ten feet before me, short and round and dark. Like a man crouching.

Like Grim taking a moment to recover.

"Grim," I murmured, taking a step closer to the shadow.

The form moved, growing darker, its transparency lessening until I could see the shape of the man who'd been my guide through all of this. Who'd pushed me and dragged me and saved me and had lain on top of me just the day before. Whom I knew as rough, mean, and the best kisser I'd ever had the honor of kissing back. Until I saw Grim exactly as I'd assumed—crouching on the ice, seeming to catch the breath he did not need.

"Grim, are you okay?"

The man appeared from the smoke, solid and sure, staring at the ice below him as his entire body rocked with the effort of being still. Winner of the fight, it seemed, though I could see scratches on his skin. Could see dark patches along the side of his face. He looked like a man who'd been in a brutal battle and almost lost. Almost been beaten.

I fought back worried tears and took a single step in his direction. "Grim—"

My breath caught as he jerked his head up, his eyes staring right through me. Black eyes glowing in the shadows of dusk. But I had seen those before; that wasn't what made my world go completely sideways and the terror of the situation come to squeeze the air out of my lungs.

No, it wasn't the glowing eyes that made me realize how much danger I was in.

The black goo dripping slow and thick from the corner of his mouth did that. The black goo like what the wraith had dripped onto the concrete seemingly so long ago. This time, it came from Grim, though. The man whom I'd allowed close to me. Whom I'd kissed.

The man whom I had thought was different from those trying to steal my soul.

My scream overpowered the cracking of the ice and made the air stand still.

CHAPTER

SIXTEEN

THE ARRIVAL

"Witch, stop."

There would be no stopping, not for a creature that dripped the corrosive, black goo from their mouth. I hadn't expected to see that from Grim, hadn't been ready for it. But once I saw the horror in real time, the wall I'd been slowly building flew up between us. The bones had shown me a betrayal—it had come. Grim wasn't the man I had thought he was. He wasn't a *man* at all, which I had known from the start, but I hadn't thought he was like the wraiths who had attacked me. Who had bitten my arm and caused my brain to go fuzzy. Or had that been Grim's very presence messing with my mind? I couldn't have known, but it had to be one of them. All of them—Hypnos and Death himself included. Or maybe Grim was death…or Death. Or…something.

By the Goddess, the confusion inside me only made me angrier.

"Witch—"

"You're just like *them*!" I yelled, not slowing down in the slightest.

"Not really."

"That's not a no."

"I am a reaper, and they are not. It's as simple as that."

Rage burned through me. Scarlett the fire witch would have had the ends of her hair on fire if she'd felt as mad as I did. I wasn't powerful enough with fire to make anything on my body burn, but I did cause a small tornado to form on the ice between the two of us. I was oddly proud of that little wind geyser. At least until Grim stomped right through it, destroying it like he had my trust in him.

Oh, but to be able to set the ends of my hair on fire.

"Witch, stop."

"You keep saying that and I keep not stopping, so you might as well hold your tongue." I glanced in his direction, making sure to keep my face pinched and hard. "If you're trying to kill me, you'll fail."

"You're already dead."

It was beyond irritating when people were technically right but in a way that was oblivious to the point of their wrongness. "You know what I mean."

Grim grabbed me, nearly pulling me off my feet as he yanked me into his arms. His dark eyes glowed again, and his growl rumbled in his chest. He looked as if he'd surrendered to his other side. All animal or demon or…something not human. And that creature fought to hold on to me.

I saw no black goo on his lips as he said, "If I had wanted to devour your soul, little witch, I already would have."

The growl in his voice, the tightness of his hands on me. They brought forth memories of the previous night. Of being held down by him, pleasured by him. Owned by him. My attraction flared just as hot and bright as my anger, adding to the latter and inflating my confusion. I wanted to shove him away and pull him closer, wanted to punch him and kiss him at the same time. The man bewildered me, leaving me lost in the gravity of him without my cards to guide me.

But I had to break that spell…no matter what. So I reached for the first divisive subject that came to mind. "Who is that man following us?"

Grim balked, his face screwing up for a moment before settling back into his angry countenance. "He's not your concern."

Disappointing and absolutely maddening. I'd been with the demigod for days, had shared my stories. Sure, I had learned a little about him, but not enough. And especially not about the creatures around us I felt were a threat to me. Grim just kept me in the dark, and I was tired of it.

I pulled myself out of his hold, shaking my head. "Then I have to assume you—and he—are like the wraiths. You are not safe for me."

"You are maddening, witch."

"And you are a monster."

Grim froze, those words seeming to hit him like a physical force. Something in his body language, something in his expression, gave away how much my calling him that hurt. I'd landed a direct hit without even trying.

And I felt guilty as hell about it.

"Grim—"

"Keep walking," he said, his voice rough and low. Angry. "It'll be full dark soon."

He stomped past me, heading for the land before us. He'd led the way countless times over the past few days, but this felt different. There was something in his stride, in his posture, that screamed surrender. He was leaving me behind, and that wasn't like him.

I hurried after him, questions and doubts and worries swirling through my mind where the cards should have been. My thoughts making patterns in the mist filling that side of my brain. I was being gaslit—I knew that. I had seen the man drip the ooze with my own eyes, had witnessed how alike he was to those wraiths that had tried so very hard to kill me. Or devour me. Or whatever would happen, seeing as how I was already dead. I had *seen* it.

But Grim looked like a man who'd just had his feelings hurt, and that meant I'd done something wrong.

Being undead in the land of the dead was super confusing.

Grim made it to land before me, standing tall and proud on the embankment as I crawled up after him. He didn't offer to help me, didn't reach out a hand, which was again very different for him. I was halfway ready to apologize, to start a conversation so we could find our way through this, when my feet hit the solid ground on the top of the hill.

Energy. Strong and fierce and filled with witchcraft and magick. It enveloped me, knocking me to my knees as the strength of our ancestors pulsed through what was left of my soul. There was no looking past it or ignoring it, no doubt in my mind what it meant. I let out a single sob of relief, not having prepared for the reunion of our powers. Not ready to be so close yet.

"Witch?" Grim stood over me, his feet right at the edge of my vision field. Sounding concerned. But this moment, this feeling, had nothing to do with him. This was pure witch energy. This was Weaver magick.

"She's here." I pushed off the ground, welcoming the energy of the elements inside. Supporting it with my body language. I gave the sigil on my damaged hand—the one the ancestor had burned into my flesh—a rub, giggling as it lit up. As it burned. Fire. Smoldering embers under my darkened, sickly skin. Only one witch could share her power with me in a way to let the flames build within me. That set me on fire from the inside out. "She's alive. My sister is here, and she's still alive."

I was running before I finished my sentence, following the energy across the island. Scarlett was close, her power a physical force. Her elemental magick coating the entire island like a force field. I had made it.

Now all I had to do was save her life. Again.

CHAPTER SEVENTEEN

THE BETRAYAL

I needed no map or directions to find my sister—I never had. Our magick cast a wide net with a pull to the source that drew me to her as only our bond could do. I could feel her presence, sense her location through the vibrations around me, so I followed that sensation. Through the deserted streets and up onto the bluff overlooking the lake, I ran without pause. Without slowing down. I kept my feet moving, basking in the glow of sisterly connections. Of Weaver magick.

I ran toward where I knew Scarlett had to be until bad luck and dark energy forced me to a standstill.

I had just crested another hill, making a turn more inward on the island, when the shadow man appeared before me. He wasn't shadowy anymore, though. He looked a lot like Grim—hard and solid, mean, with glowing eyes and dark lips. Almost black, to be honest, a sharp contrast to his grayed-out skin. I shivered at the memory of the goo sizzling as it hit concrete. As it dripped from Grim's lips. The four were obviously connected somehow, and it had become time to find out how.

"Who are you?"

The shadow man—Hypnos—cocked his head, a cruel sort of smile curling one side of his mouth upward. "Grim hasn't told you?"

"No. He says it's none of my business."

"That's an interesting opinion, considering your situation."

I was about to ask what he meant by that when Grim ran over the top of the hill, growling deeply as he stormed right past me. "Stay away from her."

Hypnos kept his eyes locked on me as he said, "You have a job to do."

A slow headshake from Grim caught my attention, a tightening of his muscles some may not have even noticed. "Not with her."

Her being me, though I had no idea what job Grim had to do for me. Or would it be to me? Against me? None of this was good news or particularly informative, but I kept my mouth shut. Kept watching the two creatures as they faced off.

Hypnos finally looked away from me, scowling at Grim. "They won't like being denied such a tasty treat."

"Who are they?" I asked, needing info. I assumed the they were the wraiths. The two forms who had attacked me a few times at the start of the trip. But still, I needed confirmation because there could be other theys.

Both men ignored me, though. Grim even went on speaking as if he hadn't heard me.

"I'll handle them. Just stay out of our way."

Hypnos coughed a deep laugh and disappeared into a smoky mist, reforming directly in front of me. That close—right up in my face—he looked so much more like Grim. Same skin color, same harsh bone structure, same full lips. They even had the exact same eyes. Like Scarlett, Azurine, and me. So different but the same. Sisters.

Brothers.

Hypnos reached out and dragged a finger over my cheek, leaning in to whisper, "I can smell them in you."

The world exploded in my head, the cards flipping madly even though I couldn't see their images. One word stood out to me—in. He had said *in*, as in inside. He could smell *them inside* me. The only them I could even contemplate were the wraiths, which meant that bite, the coldness and the heat that grew from it, the fact that I hadn't felt my hand in days, meant far worse things than Grim had told me.

As if my thoughts called to him, Grim appeared before me, shoving Hypnos out of the way with a roar.

"Stay away from her."

"Tell her."

"I'll handle it."

Hypnos took a step back, his eyes coming to meet mine once more. "Tell her, or I will."

I looked over at Grim, whose expression matched his name. "Grim, please."

"No," he said, growling louder. His energy deep and dark and angry. "Hyp—"

"Tell her!"

But Grim said nothing in response to the demand. He stood silent instead, his head hanging. Looking like a man about to surrender. About to lose. Looking so very defeated.

He broke my heart. "Grim?"

But Hypnos didn't give him a chance to respond to me. "The bite is impossible to stop. Your soul is being dissolved from the inside of your form. You'll be one of us soon, though in a much more painful way than if my brother here had simply… taken what was his and finished the job."

Out of all the words he'd spoken, out of all the horrible things flying through my head, I became stuck on one simple phrase. *What was his*. Rage brewed within me, and the earth responded with a deep rumble as a strong, howling wind blew across the bluff. Three small vortices formed around me, stirring up sand and dust. Lifting my hair with their power.

I wasn't on fire, but I had a feeling I looked a little scary.

"I belong to no one."

Hypnos cocked his head again, his face serious as he looked me over. "Oh, sweet little witch. You've been his since he first saw you back when you were alive. Why do you think—with all those people at the Merriweather battle—there was no way for you to survive?"

The air went still, the entire world going silent. My mouth fell open as his words reverberated through my brain. As the possibility that I had been played by Grim for far longer than I'd thought possible settled into my reality. It couldn't be. The cards would have told me. Percy would have seen something. My own mother, long dead and living in the Summerlands, would have known and told me when I arrived.

As I stood and tried to make sense of the level of betrayal perpetrated against me, Grim took a more direct approach. He raced at Hypnos, the two slamming into each other and shifting smokelike again. I had no doubt this time about what the two had become engaged in, though. They had begun a battle in the sky, and I no longer cared who won.

Cards flipping but unseeable, future unknown but not impossible, I walked right past the two fighting clouds and headed for the energy of my sister. I nearly huffed a laugh as the smoke in my visions rose and darkened, as it thickened. Looking like Grim and Hypnos in their non-corporeal forms. I ignored them, though, because my brain had filled with firing synapses as all the information permeated me. Of course, the cards were no longer visible to me—my soul was dying, which meant whatever energy Grim and Hypnos and the wraiths had was overwhelming my witch side. Not completely, seeing as how I still had my powers, but partially. Almost picking and choosing what to destroy first or possibly picking off the weakest of my gifts.

The loss of my foresight sort of made sense, though. Grim's response to it…it did as well, but it also hurt. A lot. All that time, the days of me stressing over not being able to see the cards, Grim likely knew exactly why that was. He had chosen not to tell me, which constituted being untrue in my mind. He had lied to me. He had allowed my gift to weaken and be overtaken instead of telling me what was happening. I might have had options had I known what was coming, might have been able to call the corners or seek deeper, darker magick to fight whatever was going on inside my body.

I could have done *something* if I'd have understood the danger I was in, but Grim had said nothing so I would die. Again. This time without the option of reincarnation. Without my family by my side. Without anyone to grieve for me. He had left me the night of the attack, even after promising he wouldn't, and allowed the wraith to take her bite. To begin my second death. He had set this up.

"Little witch, stop."

Oh, but there would be no listening to his orders. Not today, not tomorrow, not ever again. "Whatever will happen to me is already in motion, but that won't stop me from saving my sister. I have a job to do."

"Witch—"

I spun as his hand brushed my elbow, glaring hard, my rage a physical force. A scream to the Goddess. A call to the corners for their help. Without saying an actual word, they responded.

A gust of wind blew past me, streamlined to the point to hit only Grim, knocking him down with its force. The air kicked up sand and leaves, branches and debris all around me, swirling in a protective circle that built upon itself. That continued up into the sky, not even beginning to slow until it stood ten feet high. The energy of the earth did not disappoint either. It rose through my feet at the same time, my secondary power building. My balance solid and strong.

My ancestors had heard my cry, knew my need, and had responded. I would need to offer my thanks at some point, but right then, I had a demigod to deal with.

I slammed my foot down onto the sandy soil, and the vortex collapsed, all the debris floating in the air falling to the ground as the earth gave one solid rumble. As Grim stared at me with something akin to terror in those glowing eyes. My show of power had caused the man to be afraid of me.

Good.

"My name is Amber, not little witch, and I will not allow you to run this show. I am here for my sister, not you. Leave me alone."

With that, I turned on my heel and jogged down the road, tears burning my eyes as all the losses I'd been forced to endure in my short life and even shorter afterlife piled up in my head. As I remembered all the decisions along the way, all the challenges I had been given. Somewhere, somehow, Grim had been involved in many of them, and the fact that I had no idea when my free will had been cut short and his power play had begun gutted me.

My life had not been my own for a very, very long time.

I slowed and grabbed my arm, the heat pulsing there. The knowledge of what was happening in that limb turning my stomach. I had no idea how much longer I had as myself, how soon my soul would be dissolved as Hypnos had said, if I even had a shot at making it back to the Summerlands so my mother and ancestors could attempt to heal me, but it didn't matter. Not really. I'd already lost everything once—my family, my friends, and my life.

Once I saved Scarlett from whatever fate was heading her way, I could lose it all again and continue on to my eternal death knowing I had done my best.

So long as I won against whatever was coming to kill her, I would be okay.

I hoped.

CHAPTER

EIGHTEEN

THE RELEASE

Grim was not one to take direction well. In fact, when I told him to leave me alone, what he apparently heard was "stalk my every step across the island and continually attempt to acquire my attention."

"Witch. Stop and talk to me."

See?

But even though Grim tried to distract me, my mind remained focused. Raging and conflicted about what to do with the specter behind me, but fixated on my sister. I stormed up the hill to Scarlett's house as if I could stop whatever was going to happen with nothing more than my presence. As if just showing up would right the world and Scarlett would be saved.

When I reached the top, though, my concentration faltered. The view of Scarlett's house in the shadowy forest stole it, snagging me with its stunning vista. I had to pause to take it all in. The trees, the lush foliage—washed-out but still impressive—the lake off in the distance. So much beauty to absorb, so many details to take note of.

I'd never seen Scarlett's house in the real world when I'd been alive. My sister and her mate had bought their home here after their twins were grown, so I'd only ever caught glimpses of it through my cards while trying to keep an eye on her. The house was much bigger than I'd expected, with a deep, wrap-around porch and dark wood trim. Signs of the witchlings she took in—children and teenagers thrown out of their homes either because the parents were afraid of their powers or because they were from witch covens and the families didn't think they were powerful enough—decorated the windows and property. A bike here, a piece of stained glass likely made from a kit hanging from a single window, a stuffed toy in a rocking chair. All normal things.

The pentagrams carved into the porch posts could be considered a little less normal, as were the runes decorating the edge of the porch trim. Specific flower and herb plants filled the beds—out of place for a traditional landscape but totally normal in the witch world. Lavender, rosemary, calendula—all within the front beds along the porch. No pretty flowers, just powerful plants needed in everyday spell craft. This was a witch's home, for sure.

The entire property carried the energy of magick, and it looked the part as well. The house stood stately and yet a little on the spooky side, especially since the evening had begun to turn into full night, leaving us all in a space of shadows. A glow shone through the windows, making the house appear occupied and filled with love, but the deepening darkness of that wide porch left it slightly reserved as well. I would have stared at this house if I'd driven by it, enamored with all the details. I also wouldn't have wanted to stop and knock on the door for fear of what might answer. It fit Scarlett to a T.

The wind picked up as I thought of my sister, my element responding to the emotions building within me. A wave of my sister's energy danced along my skin, and I sighed at the warmth it imbued. Scarlett—the fire witch. Wildest of the three of us but also likely the most talented. The smartest. The one with the biggest heart. Didn't matter the threat—the girl always came out swinging. She had been our protector from day one. By the Goddess, had I missed her. I practically vibrated with my need to see her. Wishing she would step outside onto that porch and show herself to me. I hadn't seen a living person's essence in the realm between, but I hoped. I prayed to the Goddess that I would be allowed to see her. That I could help her.

Unfortunately, it wasn't Scarlett who I saw next. It was Grim after he caught up to me on the ridge. The man moved as if to grab my arm—the good one, not the one slowly killing me all over again—but I yanked it away from him.

"Don't touch me."

Grim was not one to be deterred. "You need to listen to me."

"What I need to do is save my sister's life."

"And how exactly do you plan to do that when you don't even know what it is you're protecting her from?"

Fair point, but also one that increased the anger inside me. "Well, I would know if I hadn't have been bitten by your sisters."

"They're not my sisters."

I took a step forward, so angry the wind had begun to swirl around us. "I don't believe you."

"Yes, you do. Whether you want to or not, you trust me."

Oh, the gall of that man. My rage grew deeper, stronger, the wind streaming harder and louder around us, howling as it came screaming in off the water.

"You're wrong," I said, my voice louder than usual. Not yelling, just more forceful to be heard over the wind. "I don't trust you. I don't want you around me anymore. In fact, maybe I should just blow you right off the bluff."

I spread my arms wide and dropped my head to look at the sky, yelling a spell to call the corners into play. The wind picked up and the earth itself began to shimmy, but Grim was not deterred. He grabbed me mid-spell and yanked my arms down, holding me in place. Forcing me into his embrace even as I tried to fight him off.

"You need to quit fighting against me, witch."

The waves grew higher out on the lake, crashing below us on the bluff as my anger made them swirl and pound the shore. "My name is not witch."

"I will call you what I want until you calm the hell down."

"I'm not calming down—my sister—"

"Your sister is out of your control!" Grim screamed, obviously trying to be heard over the roar of the world growing around us.

"My sister needs me!" I screamed back, feeling the elements coming together. My hair blowing wildly around my head in the wind. "I am the only one who can help to save her life."

"Your sister is in the realm of the living. There is nothing you can do for her from here."

From here... From the Reversed. The land of the dead and yet not the final resting place for them. From the place none of us belonged. The wind died down, the earth going still beneath our feet. His words had landed in a way I hadn't been prepared for.

"If I can't possibly help her, why did you come along with me?" I watched as Grim flinched, as his face went hard and stoic. As he tried to hide the truth from me once more. But I was no longer blinded by him, no longer willing to accept his words and actions as truth. I knew better.

And still, this betrayal stung.

"You were just waiting for me to fail."

He shook his head, a slow and deliberate motion. "No."

But it was too late—the pieces had begun to fall into place in my mind, and I didn't need the cards to see what had been happening around me.

"You watched me through the door. You… coveted me. You waited for me to find a reason to cross into this hellscape." I tried to push out of his hold, but he only tightened his grip, making me huff as my frustration hit a boiling point. "What is it you want from me?"

"Not from you. Just you."

Of course. He wanted me, had always wanted me. "You killed me, didn't you?"

Grim's face screwed up, a horrified look taking over his handsome features. "No. That wasn't me."

"You helped."

"I didn't. I was there, but I had nothing to do with your end."

"You could have stopped it, though," I choked out, shaking my head. "You could have stepped in so I didn't die."

Grim went still and quiet, staring at me. Giving pause before saying, "There is no stopping Death."

Oh, how wrong he was. "I did. I stopped him once. I could have done it again."

"Amb—"

"You could have told me what I was up against." I closed my eyes, pretending not to have heard my name on his lips. Needing to have no memory of the way the first syllable sounded coming out of his mouth. Not now. Not after everything. "You could have kept me safe."

"I *am* going to keep you safe."

"Here."

He froze, his frown deepening. “What?”

“You’re going to keep me safe *here*.”

His brow furrowed, his irritation and confusion clear. “Of course.”

“That’s the problem. I don’t belong here. I belong in the Summerlands with the other witches.”

His face fell, shattered, really, as if he hadn’t even considered that I might want to go back. That I might not take that option. With a huff, he turned away from me, hiding his pain, but I’d seen it. I knew he hadn’t been ready for me to refuse him. And maybe—in another time or another place—I wouldn’t have. Maybe I would have agreed to stay with him had I known everything from the start. But at that point, it was too late. There were only two things I needed to say.

“You betrayed my trust.”

Grim grunted, an angry sound as he turned those hard devil eyes to mine. “You were perfectly happy accepting my help.”

As if his betrayal was earned because of such a thing. That only fueled my need to get one last thing off my chest.

I bent down to unwrap the piece of his shroud from my ankle, rising with it in my hand. Offering it to him. "Call in your favor."

He stared at the cloth in my hand for a long time, eyes hard and angry. "You don't want to—"

"I'm done." I tossed the fabric at him, not caring that it fell to the ground. That it lay discarded at our feet. "Call in your favor."

His face scrunched, his head cocking as if confused. "What favor?"

"You said you would get me here for a favor to be decided upon later. Call it in."

"Witch—"

But I was done being nice. I stood my ground, feet planted on my Mother Earth, speaking my truth into the falling night. "I'm here. I can save her. I don't need you. Call in your favor and go."

Something about my words hit home, because Grim sagged and dropped his head. Looking defeated for the first time since I met him. Looking like a man who had given up.

"I release you from our deal."

And with that, he turned and walked back down the bluff. Leaving me behind.

Walking away from the damage he'd caused.

CHAPTER NINETEEN

THE FAMILY

Night moved in as she always did, intensifying the shadows under the trees and leaving the house surrounded by blackness. Only the lights burning inside Scarlett's place illuminated my approach. Dead leaves crunched under my feet. The wind continued to caress my skin, following me up the last of the hill to the home of my youngest sister.

The house sat silent and still in the evening shadows, the roofline so drastically pitched and far over my head as to be invisible. I would have called it Victorian and likely been wrong, but that sort of feeling filled me as I approached. The white cladding, the black trim around the windows and doors, the same black paint on the porch floor, all very old-fashioned and timeless but with moldings that added details to place the structure in a particular time frame.

The porch lay deep and extra dark, but there was something about it that called to me. Something that stood out in a world of gray the way it shouldn't have. That porch had a haint-blue ceiling. The color—a soft, light blue—purportedly mimicked the sky and was supposed to confuse ghosts and spirits before they made their way inside. Using the color wasn't from our sect of witchcraft, but it added a bit of whimsy to the porch. A bit of multicultural magick to the place. And told me the paint worked since I was definitely in the land of the dead and very confused by how I could see the color in the first place.

Off to one side of the porch, what looked like a small, metal tree—maybe five feet tall and branching every few inches—stuck out of the ground. Cobalt blue bottles hung from the branches, each glinting in the fading light of the setting sun. Another bit of magick not from our family, another tool to keep the spirits away. Another spot of color in the gray landscape. Someone truly didn't like ghosts and was definitely digging deep into that druid-like, Appalachian magick.

I had to chuckle to myself as I looked around, though—the blues were there and surprising, but definitely not working. At least, not the way they were intended to. I had no fear of the blue, no real confusion. What I had was the unwanted memory of Grim's blue eyes as I looked over those bottles. The warmth that color had imbued in me. The remembrance of blue eyes on mine as he had pleasured me with his body.

"Stupid memories," I whispered, physically shaking off the energy of such thoughts.

Picturing Grim's blue eyes staring down at me was not the way to save my sister.

I took a deep breath and refocused my mind on Scarlett, absolutely locking away all the emotions left over from my dealings with Grim, seeking my sister's energy instead. There was so much power in this little pocket of the world, so much magick. It danced across my skin and sent tingles up the back of my neck. A witch called this property hers, pure and simple. The entire land had to have been warded for me to feel so much energy without seeking it, which meant Scarlett had been hard at work to protect her space. Or maybe it had been one of the other witches—one of her abandoned witchlings—needing the security of clean energy and barriers to those who might harm them. Either way, the space felt like home. Something I craved after—

Well, just *after.*

Needing to be sure my sister was fine, wanting so badly to actually see her face, I opened my mind to her. Letting pictures flow through my brain, letting memories I had been tucking away for safekeeping come out to play. Us together on the lake as children, making trouble and laughing about it. Late nights under blankets, all three of us piled into one bed as we told one another ghost stories and whispered secrets. The fear and anger on her face when I had stayed silent after setting the back porch on fire, having known she'd be the one blamed since she was the fire witch of the family. Little bits and moments, all dancing across my brain and filling me with joy.

But light cannot shine without darkness. Other pictures crept through my parade of memories as well. Bad ones. Ones I'd rather avoid. Past mistakes I'd made regarding her and Azurine, decisions I'd long regretted.

My past berated me, weakening my resolve. Making me feel like a failure. The wind, though—she whipped past me, stirring up leaves and making the branches of the trees swing down toward me. Reminding me of why I had come. Of the future that had played out behind my eyes with my sister lying dead and gray on the ground. Grim's demon face, eyes glowing and black ooze dripping from his lips. Big hands on my body and the way he—

"No." I shook my head, trying to rid myself of the memories. "Not anymore. Keeping Scarlett alive is my priority."

Without fear of being confused by the haint-blue ceiling, I stepped onto Scarlett's porch. Wanting to be closer to her. Wishing I could see her through a window or something. I assumed I could walk in—it wasn't like what I did in this realm directly affected the living—but some witch had taken great care in warding the space from spirits. I would not be the one to disrespect their magick and break their barriers. If Scarlett was in danger, of course, but the house felt calm and peaceful. No sign of danger apparent. I would continue to respect my sisters in magick and stay outside. For now.

I was walking along the railing, still seeking my sister's energy, when the front door opened, and a young woman walked out with a phone pressed to her ear.

"Yeah, I know. Everything's fine, though."

I gasped, my entire body locking into place. For the briefest of moments, it was as if I'd been transported back through time. Back to when the three of us Weaver sisters had reached the ripe old age of twenty-one and thought we were ready to take on the world. The girl on the porch was the spitting image of my sister Azurine, from the dark hair to the strong cheekbones, to the way she just seemed to take up so much space with her energy. The woman was a Weaver through and through.

"You don't need to come up here. The ferries aren't running, and you know Mom and Dad will throw an absolute hissy fit if you dare to step foot on the ice bridge. Just stay at school. I'll take care of anything that comes up and let you know if you're needed."

Creeping in a circle around her, I began to notice the differences between her and my sister. Azurine's hair had always been deep and dark in color, but this girl's had a lighter tinge in segments. Streaks of color not natural in the human realm, almost like stripes. I wondered if they were dyed red like Scarlett's or lighter—near blond, perhaps.

She turned, and I got a solid look at her face. Her eyes weren't like Azurine's either. They were wider, less almond-shaped and more catlike, with a sharpness that cut through space even in the reverse.

"Stay safe, Ginge. I'll be back in a few days."

Ginge. Ginger. Which meant this young lady, who looked so much like a Weaver that it hurt, had to be the twin sister, Poppy. My dead heart broke in two as I looked her over, all that I'd missed during my time in the Summerlands standing before me. I wouldn't have known which twin she was, wouldn't have been sure she wasn't a child of Azurine's, had I not heard her on the phone. I still didn't—not really. I was making assumptions because I'd never met her.

Because I'd died before she was born. Before I'd even known my sister to be pregnant.

Oh, to be able to see her in the daylight of the living realm just for a moment. To be able to absorb every detail of the beauty my sister had borne.

As I grappled with a sense of loss so profound it made me feel as if the earth were shifting beneath my feet, the door opened again. This time, the person who walked out was someone I knew. Someone I had met. Someone I recognized.

"I brought you some tea." Shadow—Scarlett's red thread or fated partner—smiled at his daughter before handing the girl a steaming cup and wrapping an arm around her shoulders. "How's your sister?"

The girl sighed, cupping the mug in her hands. "She's fine. Worried like the rest of us, but fine."

"Your mother will be fine."

"She doesn't seem fine."

Shadow looked out toward the bluff, likely focusing on the water, still as young and handsome as the day we'd met. Which had to be over two decades before, maybe more, depending on when exactly the twins had come. So much time lost. So much…missed.

"Your mother misses her sister," Shadow said, his voice calm and quiet. Almost as if sharing a secret.

"But Aunt Zuri said—"

"Not Azurine. Her other sister."

Me. They were worried about Scarlett because she missed me. Oh, my soul. It exploded right there. A thousand pieces shattering in silence.

"Right. I forgot about her." The girl's shoulders slumped, her attention brought back to the mug. "I hate when she gets like this."

"We all do, but grief is not something one ever gets over. It hunts you, haunts you, and in the quietest of moments, consumes you once more."

My poor Scarlett, missing me just as much as I missed her. As I'd done a thousand times, I wished that I'd had more time with my family. More time with the living. I wished I would have been more than *her* to the young woman standing before me—a character in the stories likely told at family gatherings, with no true memories attached. I'd made the decision to sacrifice myself so my sisters could find their forever happiness, but I hadn't considered how much the loss of me in their lives would affect them. Hadn't considered the ripples through the generations my sudden death would cause. If Scarlett felt half the pain I did in that moment, she was suffering. Deeply.

"What can I do to help her?" the girl asked, her voice barely more than a whisper.

But her dad—the shifter with two parts, wolf and tiger—heard her just as clearly as I had. "Love her, my sweet Poppy. That's all. Love her through this moment, and she'll be okay. She's just sad."

He hugged her tighter, the two snuggling together in the shadows of the evening. A familial island in the sea of this life. I sniffed, fighting to hold back tears, and started to creep backward. This was a moment between parent and child, one I wasn't meant to see. One that should have been private. Poppy—one of the nieces I had never met—needed the support of her father, and I would give her the privacy to take that from him.

But as I took a step, Shadow's head jerked up, his eyes zeroing in on me. Or at least pinpointing where I stood. My entire body froze, locked in place by the animallike gaze. His stare pierced my skin, something dark and familiar rolling through my blood. A simple look that had nothing simple about it. He couldn't see me—he wasn't looking me in the eye—but he could sense me.

And while perhaps that moment should have brought me joy, should have made me feel a part of their world, it did the opposite. Shadow staring through me made me feel even more disconnected from the realm of the living than ever before. He couldn't see me—not in this form. Not with us in two different realms.

No one could see me.

No one but Grim.

And I didn't want that man around me.

CHAPTER TWENTY

THE BROTHER

I spent the night on the porch, sleeping fitfully through the darkest hours with my rucksack under my head. Why the dead even needed to sleep consumed my mind in the quiet of the resting period, though I was too tired to truly contemplate an answer. Dead tired, if I was being punny. Grim would have grunted a response to that one—not a laugh, just an accepting guttural sound of satisfaction. Not that I ended up thinking of him in the few moments when my mind finally went quiet and still. Not at all.

Eventually, I woke to a cold and dreary morning, mist falling from the sky. The dampness in the air made my arm hurt worse than ever, made the numbness seem to sink deeper than before. I pulled up my cardigan sleeve, wanting to cry when I saw how shrunken and destroyed my forearm had become, how the black lines spidering off from the bite had turned my fingertips the same inky color and run up over my elbow. Death had been spreading, and it hurt. A lot. The pain was something I hadn't been expecting, and I hissed as I tried to stretch out my hand.

"That won't help."

I jumped at the male voice coming from a pocket of shadows at the back of the porch, not relaxing when a man strolled from them as if he'd been standing there waiting for me to wake up. Which he likely had.

The shadow man had found me again.

"Been watching me sleep?" I asked, faking a bravado I did not feel. "That's creepy, you know."

"And the fact that you still sleep at all is weird."

My face drew tight, my lips certainly pulling into a frown as my brain once again spun sideways on that particular subject. "I was actually thinking that last night."

"Then I guess you're not completely hopeless."

"Gee, thanks." I stared down at my hands, comparing the two. One normal if not slightly gray, the one darker, with deep, black lines like veins snaking up and down it, the color pooling at the ends. Life and death. Or death and… further death. All of which should have been explained to me at some point by… "How is he?"

I didn't need to specify the *he*.

"You shouldn't be worried about him. You made a mistake trusting him."

As if I needed *that* spelled out for me. "You think I don't realize my error?"

"Realize it, and yet you still show concern for my brother. Why?"

"Because I'm not a monster?"

"Neither are we, witch." He moved closer, crouching down to be eye level with me. "He lied to you, deceived you, hid the truth from you, and yet you worry over his state. I do not understand this."

"He made sure I got here in one piece."

He nodded toward my darkened arm. "That's debatable."

I tugged my cardigan sleeve back over my hand, hiding the damage.

"And what? You think I should trust you instead? That your words carry any weight with me? Because I've got to be honest—you seem cut from the same cloth as Grim." I reached for the edge of his shroud, lifting then releasing a section of gauzy fabric at his wrist. "Literally."

"Grim and I are not the same. He is weak, unable to do the job required of us without complaint. He bends the rules to fit his whims and expects forgiveness instead of punishment. He is—"

"Better than you." The words came naturally, almost automatically. An understanding running deep within my body. The ancestors agreed, sending the morning sunlight to dapple the ground in front of the steps and a cool breeze across the porch. If Grim was not to be trusted, Hypnos was not to be believed. I could feel that coming from the basest of instincts I had.

Hypnos growled, his eyes glowing like Grim's sometimes would as his anger made its appearance. "What did you say to me, witch?"

I rose to my feet, sighing. Pushing past him to walk toward the back of the house so I could look out over the water. My mind spinning over what I had heard, what I had seen, what I had a sense of. I didn't need the cards to know this about the man following behind me.

"I said Grim is better than you. What…did you expect me not to hear sour grapes in your little monologue? *He is bad, he does what he wants, he gets away with it.* The part you're missing there, friend, is the *and I can't do the same*."

"You dare to challenge me?"

I shrugged, not turning around. Not giving in to the low-level anxiety buzzing in my gut. "I don't think calling out the meaning behind your words is challenging. It's seeking the truth, which you apparently want to hide. Now, how is Grim doing?"

There was a pause, a beat of complete silence, before the sound of something whistling through the air broke it. I spun, ready to cast magick at whatever was coming my way, but stopped and froze in terror instead. A wraith had come to call, flying around Hypnos as if to embrace him. Or perhaps contain him. He certainly didn't look happy to have the smoky spirit nearby.

"Stop it, Peggy."

The wraith shifted before my eyes, becoming more solid. Becoming…humanlike. Forming into the shape of a woman. "I hate it when you call me Peggy."

Hypnos did not seem surprised by her change in form. "I'm aware."

I stood and stared, unable to believe my eyes. Not knowing whether to scream or run or…pray. What did a witch do when facing down two demons?

Though, Peggy-not-Peggy certainly didn't look very demon-like. In fact, she looked almost… normal. Long, wavy hair, petite features, gray skin with darkened spots along her cheeks as if she'd had freckles at some point in her journey. She looked like the dead version of the girl next door.

At least until she turned and stabbed me with her steely black gaze. "You're the one causing all the upset around there."

I waved, having absolutely no idea what else I could do. The move must have caught her off guard because she snorted a rough laugh.

"This one should be left alone," she said, removing her attention from me and focusing once more on Hypnos. "Grim wouldn't like it if he knew you were here."

"Then perhaps he should be minding his pet."

I opened my mouth to argue that I definitely wasn't anyone's pet, but Peggy-not-Peggy beat me to it.

"She's not a pet, and you're just cranky. Why don't you head out and go put some dying humans to rest, Hypnos? Do the job you were killed for."

"Why don't you quit wasting time on things left to the living and go devour some souls, Peggy?"

The woman smiled, the slow rise of her lips looking threatening in ways I couldn't even comprehend. Almost…animalistic. "Oh, I plan to. Yours will be first if you call me Peggy again."

"It's a valid nickname."

"Not to me. My name is Margaret."

"Margaret the wolf, sent to be a Keres sister. Perhaps if you—"

We all froze as the door to the house opened and Poppy walked through it. But she could not steal all of my attention. Something in Hypnos's body language, in the way he couldn't tear his eyes from my niece, sent ice shooting up my spine. I waited and watched, concern growing under the surface of my skin, until he did exactly what I knew he would. He took a single, almost unconscious step in her direction.

Oh, hell no.

"Don't," I said, the energy of my magick building around me as I pulled on the Weaver ancestors to protect one of our own. "Don't even look at her."

The wraith—Margaret—laughed, the sound sarcastic. "Well, well, well. Isn't this just quite the pickle you've found yourself in, Hypnos?"

Hypnos growled deep and low, not tearing his eyes away from an oblivious Poppy for a single moment. "Mind your business before I go back for that mate you're always crying about."

Margaret went stock-still for the briefest of seconds before exploding into smoke once more. This time, when the smoke coagulated into a form, the shape was no longer human. In fact, it was canine. Doglike.

Or perhaps, wolf.

The growl of the demonic beast broke the quiet of the morning, not that Hypnos seemed to notice. He continued to stare at Poppy and ignore the rest of us. I'd seen that stare before, had noticed it on the faces of my sisters' mates when they'd met. Had watched their shifter mates become solely focused on them in what would have been a worrying way had the men been human. Hypnos was not a human or a shifter; he was some sort of demigod from what I could tell, and he was obsessed.

I had a feeling those facts would not bode well for my niece.

"Leave her alone," I said, digging deep into my energy source. Whispering spells and calls for deities and elements in my mind.

Hypnos scoffed, still not looking away. "You have no power over me, witch."

"Maybe not," I said, raising my arms overhead as the wind began to pick up. "But that doesn't mean I won't try."

I closed my eyes, ancient languages bubbling up through my mind as I allowed the ancients to use me for sight. With a whispered three-word spell and all the intention I could muster, I stomped my foot onto the porch floor. "So I will it, so it will be."

The move would have brought more responses had I been on solid ground to connect with the earth, but the magick within me didn't disappoint. The island seemed to shake, all beings on the porch—including Poppy—looking around in fear of the source. I hated scaring the girl, but Hypnos needed to be put in his place. Needed a reminder of just what could happen when you messed with a witch. When you took on magick as old as ours.

As the earth quieted once more, an icy blast blew in off the lake, the element of air taking her turn. The gust sent the bottle tree toppling and made the screen door bang against its frame. It also made Hypnos stumble to one side, his arm reaching out to grab hold of the house. He jerked back the second his hand made contact, staring at the offending wall with something close to rage in his expression. I laughed—I knew the place had been warded. He couldn't touch the building itself, which likely also meant he couldn't go inside. Which gave me an idea.

"Go, Poppy," I said, pushing the words across the air and hoping against hope the girl had some sort of psychic ability to hear them. "Inside. Now."

There was a pause, a stiffening of her body for the smallest moment, but then Poppy raced inside the house, escaping the possibility of Hypnos trying something he shouldn't. The man himself finally turned to face me, still shaking out his arm as if he'd been shocked, looking rage-filled and ready to kill. Too bad I was already dead.

"Get in my way again, witch, and I'll devour Grim's soul myself. Punishments be damned."

The air immediately went still, the entire forest around the house going dead silent as my mind went dark. As my thoughts turned far more dangerous than I had ever expected. He would devour Grim's soul? Steal him from this land… from me? I might not have been happy with the demigod, but Hypnos's threat went too far.

Fury burned within me, making my voice come out stronger, deeper, and far more deadly than usual as I said, "Go anywhere near Grim, and I'll burn you where you stand."

"Try it, witch." Hypnos grinned and spread his arms wide. "Cast your little spells and see how your magick is useless against me."

I shrugged, keeping my eyes locked on his. "Grim told me everything burns, even in this land of the reverse." I snapped my fingers, and an orb appeared in my palm. Glowing orange and red with hints of blue at the base, it looked the part of a fireball. Even in this grayed-out world, the colors burned clear and bright. There would be no questioning it.

Hypnos stared at the burning orb, his face going from angry and aggressive to slack and obviously strained. "You will die again, witch. And this time, it will be me standing over you instead of your protective bulldog."

With that warning still reverberating through the air, Hypnos transformed into a plume of smoke and disappeared into the forest. Margaret's wolf looked my way one time, a warning in her expression, and then she did the same. Both disappearing from view within a second.

I blew on the orb, watching it float off into the trees. The sunlight dancing off it overpowering the so-called fire to reveal its true form—a simple bubble. A melding of water and air with a little fire magick thrown in for effect. A tiny, breakable bubble representing the three Weaver sisters, something we'd learned to create as children.

A toy…that had scared off a demigod. Magick really was amazing.

I was just settling down, just releasing the energy and the elements back into the ether, when the door opened once more. This time, it wasn't Poppy who came strolling out onto the porch. Wasn't Shadow or one of the witchlings either.

No, this time, it was the woman I had come to see.

My entire world flipped upside down, and I couldn't hold back a whispered, "Scarlett."

My spoken word, the small amount of air crossing my tongue and lips, seemed to almost break through the realms, echoing across the porch in ways I had never expected. Scarlett—looking as fierce and wild as she had decades before—spun in my direction as if she had heard me. As if me calling her name had somehow reached her. And for the briefest of moments, I would have sworn it had because she didn't look through me. She didn't stare off into the distance that just happened to be behind me. No, my sister looked right at me and met my gaze.

"Amber?"

Before I could answer her, a plume of smoke hurtled through the air and onto the porch. One I recognized. One that had caused my dead body too much damage. It didn't pause in its attack, didn't give me even a second to collect myself before it struck Scarlett square in the chest. Her head fell back, and her dropping mouth opened as her eyes went wide. As her body seemed to go almost limp while still remaining upright.

Her scream bouncing off the haint-blue porch ceiling, sending the entire realm reeling.

CHAPTER TWENTY-ONE

THE FIGHT

Everyone knows about fight or flight, the two warring instincts that occur when a person is presented with a situation that leads to fear and panic. Most people don't know that there are actually two more instinctual responses. Fawn, or to show approval of your attacker—usually used by people brought up around violence and abuse—and freeze. Freeze is pretty self-explanatory. When presented with the worst-case scenario, one shuts down and refuses to fawn, fight, or take flight.

Seeing my sister being attacked by what was likely the same wraith that had bit me and destroyed my arm threw me straight into freeze.

I stood and stared, unable to move or think or process what I was seeing for barely a second—the shortest period of time in the world, really—but that was enough for the wraith to wrap itself around my sister's body and begin to…I didn't even know. Hypnos had said Margaret needed to go devour souls, and by the way Scarlett's eyes went blank, the way her entire body began to bow as the wraith tightened her hold on my sister, I had to assume that was what was happening.

Thankfully, when my brain came back online after that one-second blink, my instinctual response shifted immediately into fight mode.

"By the Goddess, let the power of Hera fill me!" I let out a yell as I spread my arms wide, welcoming the energy of the deity Hera, goddess of air. She responded to my call immediately. The wind blew in cold and wet from the lake, screaming across the porch and making the trees bend to its will. Chairs crashed to the porch floor and slid across it as leaves and sticks whipped past the railings. Scarlett fought the wraith, stumbling on her toes until she had turned into the wind. She seemed to pause for a moment, almost as if to take a breath, and then she closed her eyes. I could sense the magick pouring off her, feel the energy she had begun to work.

I could smell the scent of fire before I saw a single spark.

"Hold on, Scar." I pushed my hands forward, directing the wind her way even as I watched the ends of her hair begin to glow like embers. My sister's strength lay in her ability to control the element of fire, but the drawback of such a powerful element lay in pain. She had to set herself on fire from the inside.

The wraith—all wispy and unable to be grabbed or coldcocked—lifted off Scarlett just the slightest, but it was enough to give me a chance.

I yelled to Hera again, curling my fingers before me as I reached for my sister, twisting the wind together with her flame. The magick working together from two different realms of existence with a timeless energy.

"You can't win against us!" I screamed, hoping the wraith could hear me over the roar of the winds howling at it. "No Weaver witch fights alone."

Suddenly, Hypnos appeared at my side, almost distracting me. He leaned against a porch railing as if not at all affected by the gale around him and looking far too pleased with himself. "Told you, witch."

Without words, I stomped my foot against the porch floor, making the earth shake below us. The tremor built quickly, shaking the trees where they stood and knocking over the chairs on the far side of the porch. With a flick of my finger, I directed a gust of wind at the startled creature, making sure to have it twist around him. Hypnos lost his balance and fell backward, landing square on his butt then sliding down the stairs and to the ground below us. Blown away, which was fine with me. I needed to focus on my sister, not some demigod with a bad attitude.

My sister who had managed to set her arms on fire. The flames grew all the way to the tops of her shoulders, definitely close enough to set the wraith on fire. The creature didn't release her, though.

I didn't have a lot of options left.

"Margaret!" I screamed, still pulling on my power of air and earth, preparing to add in water to see if that could make the beast release my sister. "Let her go before we burn you into oblivion."

"That's not Margaret." Grim came rushing toward the porch from the forest, looking terrifying in his rage. Looking more like a gift than something to fear as he ran straight at his brother. A wispy, demonic wolf ran beside him, growling all the way and heading for the stairs. Margaret—the woman who had lost her mate—had come to fight with us instead of against us.

At the foot of the stairs, the wolf shifted to her wraith form, screaming into the blast of air whipping past and circling Scarlett along with her sister form. She didn't attack my sister, though. She seemed to try to wedge herself between the other wraith and Scarlett. She was fighting her own sister to save mine.

"Keep fighting, Scar!" I took a step forward, planting my feet and strengthening my stance. "I won't let you die."

"You will not win," Hypnos said, already on his feet and moving toward Grim. The two changed to their shadow forms, circling and fighting once more. Battling across the lawn and toward the forest. A welcome sight, for sure, but not my main concern. Grim would have to take care of himself.

Margaret managed to pull the wraith from my sister for a beat, but then the shadow encircled her again, bowing her body even harder and extinguishing her flames. I took another step forward, making the house shake with my power, and spread my arms wider.

"Goddess of air, hear my call. Protect my sister, her magick cannot fall. Tornadoes or cyclones or gale force winds. Our magick needs your help again."

The wind picked up, the gusts lifting the chairs and toys to throw them across the porch. Branches flew and crashed into the porch supports, and the sounds of trees cracking due to the force being thrown against them exploded in the forest. As I watched, a funnel spout formed just off the side of the house, growing longer and stronger, turning the entire sky a deeper, darker gray than before. The tail touched down somewhere in the forest, the sound of it hitting land louder than a freight train passing by.

The deities weren't playing around anymore.

"Come, Hera's gift. Come and save us all. We thank you for your help."

Just as the tornado I had called came roaring through the trees, the front door opened. Poppy took one look at her mother—which had to be a sight, considering she couldn't see the two shadows forming an almost bubble around her—and did the opposite of me. She didn't freeze, not for a single second. Instead, she roared unlike any animal I had ever heard, her entire body bowing as sparks began to fall from her fingertips.

A fire witch, like her mother.

But unlike her mother, the young woman released a field of magick so strong, it knocked me off my feet. Magick so powerful, I could only gasp and watch. The girl, still a child, really, sent out an energy field toward her mother that was stronger than anything I'd ever even heard of.

"By the Goddess," I whispered, enthralled by her. Terrified for her. A power like that, a gift so strong, would be a beacon for all sorts. Good and bad. Those who would want to witness it and those who would want to control it. To control her.

As I watched, stripes appeared on the girl's flesh. Wide, dark, and something I had definitely seen before. Just once, though. Her dad's tiger seemed to be making itself known, adding in an unstoppable sense of earth magick to the mix.

Balancing her in a way that fed her power. The girl would be unstoppable.

At least, I hoped she would be.

But I couldn't just watch Poppy's magick in action—I had to help, had to fuel the most powerful witch I had ever seen. So, I focused, and I called to the elements of air and earth, and I chanted my spell as loud as I could to show my need to the magick around me.

"Spirits of earth, I call on you to use your power in conjunction with mine. Element of air, my friend and partner, lift my words, hear my plea. Element of fire, save your daughter, charge my words, burn her free. Element of water, join our fight, wash away the wrong, come in as gift three. Element of earth, our mother and creator, ground my work, I call to thee. Spirits of earth, I call on you. Carry me through. So mote it be."

Small tornadoes formed all around the property, blowing pine needles and leaves into the air. The earth rumbled and shook as Poppy's magick mixed with mine, tree roots appearing from nowhere, alight and flaming from deep within the earth. Hypnos and Grim had stopped fighting. They stood near the forest edge, looking on in shock as all the magick Poppy and I controlled converged on the two wraiths still encircling our loved one. As it all came together and exploded into a fiery wind that set a few of the bushes and trees on fire. That lit up the porch brighter than the sun ever could and brought a flash of color into the land of the dead.

Grim had said everything could be burned. We were about to find out.

As I stood ready to watch the wraiths be destroyed, the Goddess herself whispered in my ear. I tried to fight her need, tried to ignore her demand, but she held too much power over me.

When I opened my mouth, it was not my voice that came out.

“Sweet Margaret, shifter sister born under the power of the element of earth. Escape. Now.”

One wraith flew up and away, disappearing into the trees, while the other held on, still fighting against my sister. Still draining her. I had one last option, one final call to make. A seat of power no witch called upon unless there were no other choices.

It was time to make that call.

"Blessed be the corners, the bastions of magick, and to the Goddess Hera. I call to the watchtowers now. To the foundations of all magick in the universe. The ancestral deities feeding the power forward. Come to us now. Protect our Weaver line."

My rucksack, long since forgotten about in a corner of the porch, slid across the floor to land at my feet. The bag pulsed as if something had come alive within it, the painted owl seeming to shake and writhe on the fabric. As I watched, the owl pushed away from the fabric, becoming three-dimensional. It rose into the air and spread its wings, talons out as it flew toward my sister. Into battle.

The ancestors had made sure I was prepared with that bag. More so than I could have ever known.

The owl made contact with the wraith, knocking it backward and causing part of it to dissolve in midair. Scarlett's flame burned brighter, spreading up closer to the darkness I knew we could destroy.

The fire our magick brought burned straight toward Scarlett and Poppy, lighting up the two women in full color. The flames—tinged blue with their heat—reached out and grabbed the remaining wraith. The creature screamed and flailed, but the owl flew above her, keeping her in place. The fire jumped without provocation and devoured her, absorbing the shadow right there on the porch as it continued on its journey toward the forest. Ending the battle with nothing more than some smoke and a quiet scream that barely broke through the dying wind still blowing around us.

Scarlett fell to the porch floor as the orb of fire danced toward the tree line, grasping at her throat and coughing.

"Mom!" Poppy yelled, coming to kneel beside her. "What was that?"

"I'm not sure," Scarlett said as she wrapped her arms around her daughter. The two sat there for a moment, huddled together, both clinging to the other as they faded back to the washed-out gray I had become accustomed to. As the land of the dead began to return to normal.

But then my sister looked up.

She lifted her eyes, and her gaze stabbed right into me.

"Scarlett?" I whispered, unable to even hope she might hear me. Might see me.

But then she choked out a soft, "Amber."

My entire body crumpled as I, too, fell to my knees on the dark porch floor. My entire soul lighting up with just that one word.

She saw me.

There was a moment, a few seconds of connection I couldn't have even wished for, where we sat on her porch floor—me obviously tired and her breathing hard—but both of us present. Both seeing the other. She took a good look at me, tears streaming down her face as she seemed to try to choke out words. Her eyes zeroing in on my darkened, damaged arm. Her anger coming through and the tips of her hair once again glowing.

"Hold my hand, Poppy," she croaked, the words growing stronger as she reached for her daughter's hand. The two connecting and staring straight at me as Scarlett grew louder. "Release her. Burn the poison, save the soul."

Poppy jumped in, the two of them chanting, "Burn the poison, save the soul," in unison over and over. The energy around us grew, sizzling as it bridged the distance between us. As it crisscrossed the realms.

My hand—the one that had grown so numb and looked far more dead than the rest of me—suddenly went up in flames. I jumped back, staring in a mixture of horror and fascination as the fire seemed to be absorbed, as the feeling began to return to my fingertips. The pain clawed along my damaged skin, strong but localized.

Burning right up to where my skin looked the normal gray instead of black. My entire arm from elbow to fingertips glowing as the skin cracked and black goo oozed out of it.

The moment the first drop fell to the porch, the smoke in my head cleared and my cards came back into focus. Their return stunned me so hard, I forgot the pain and raised my hand toward my face. Only stopping when the heat grew to be too much and the brightness blinded me from the world beyond. Inside my head, though, a movie played out. Pictures flipping back and forth, my gift showing me the past and the present. Where I'd made good decisions, where I'd made bad ones. And how my decision to enter the land of the dead had been what set off the chain of events leading to this moment.

Scarlett hadn't been in danger. I'd made a mistake—I'd thought about going through the door for the smallest of moments. That decision, that option, had caused the split future of what would happen if I did to play out between my mother and me. Had I not been contemplating it, had I not actually thought of entering the Reversed as a possibility, my sister would have been fine. The Keres sisters never would have found her. None of this would have happened.

Oh, how I'd failed. Grim had been right—the cards were a crutch. And this time, they'd made me fall.

"I'm so sorry," I said, my voice weak and my tears mixing with the words on my lips. "I never meant for this to happen."

The cards flipped again, this time without any decision-making on my part. Showing me a glimpse of what was to come based on someone else's choices.

I gasped and dropped my arms, staring across the porch in horror. "Poppy!"

Hypnos, already in motion, raced toward her. Grim ran right on his heels but was not close enough to stop the demigod. To get between his brother and my niece. Thankfully, Scarlett heard me and shoved her daughter, making her look up. Making her...see? Did she see the two death gods running at her? Could she? I had no idea, but she certainly seemed to know she was in danger because without a word, the woman shifted forms to what looked like a large cat. A large striped cat like a tiger but without fur. A tiger made up of water with stripes of fire mixed in. A mix of Scarlett's fire, Shadow's earth, and with the power of Azurine's water running through her. And by the way the wind danced around her, I would have guessed she had my power of air as well. Perhaps not as strong as the others, but there.

A witch balanced by all four elements.

A creature even legend hadn't yet imagined.

Powerful beings from across the globe and all the realms would come for her if they knew of her gifts. My niece was amazing and in so much danger.

"By the Goddess," I said, almost not realizing the words were dropping from my lips. Shadow rushed out the door, saw his mate on the ground, saw his daughter in her magical animal form, and roared right along with the latter. I dug deep through pain and exhaustion, pushing with all my might on my element of air. Throwing up a barrier between the demon and the girl. Hypnos ran into it, stopping for only a moment as the rebound stole his balance. That was long enough for Grim to catch up to him and yank him back into a fight. The two shadows swirled and roiled, mixing up the air and causing a negative energy spike that fed into everyone's fears.

With Shadow clutching his wife's form and Poppy curling around them both, it occurred to me that we as a family were almost in true balance. Scarlett controlled fire with a strength I had never seen before. Shadow and his shifter energy represented earth in a way that the Goddess would have approved of. Poppy obviously had a good handle on water, fire, and earth, but she lacked the control over air that I could bring. I was needed.

I crawled across the porch floor and joined my family, reaching for Scarlett's hand with my burned one. Hoping against hope this would somehow work. My hand touched hers, and she grabbed me. Connecting us. Looking right at me and choking out a soft gasp.

"Amber."

My entire body lit up from the inside, the loss I'd felt and the grief I'd been suffering under disappearing for just a moment. I had my sister with me. She could *see* me. And though there were a million things I wanted to say and do during this intense connection I was sure wouldn't last, there was only one I truly needed to.

"We have to call the corners. Now."

Scarlett nodded, her tears falling as she screamed, "Element of fire, I call to you! Answer our plea."

A pine tree exploded from within, a ball of flames blazing upward. Scarlett nodded to Shadow, who called out his part, not nearly as strong or confident as his witch wife but not bad for a man who likely had little experience with our magick.

"Element of earth, I call to you. Answer our plea."

The earth beneath the burning tree shook and cracked open, boulders appearing where none had been. Poppy was next, not even having to shift human to call on the water to join in the fight. Her roars caused the waves of the lake far below to crash louder against the rocks, and a soft rain began to fall upon the land. There was only me left, only one more corner to call on. Only one more thing I could do to save my sister and fix the mistakes I'd made.

"Element of air, I call to you!" I screamed, raising my hands—one gray, one still burning as if under the skin. "Answer our plea. Rid us of the danger presented."

A gale of high-speed wind blasted through the area, knocking the burning tree over in a sort of slow-motion crash and creating a physical barrier to the porch. The magick making the tree glow in a way that told me it wasn't only physical. Margaret—soul-devouring wraith like her sister but yet not—dropped to the ground on the other side of the tree and landed in her human form. Watching us. Hypnos and Grim hit the ground with a thud on either side of her, both becoming solid. Leaving their shadows behind. The three looking on as Mother Nature played interference between us. Between her witches and the threat.

A threat I may have been the only one to truly understand.

“Leave here, Hypnos!” I yelled, keeping my eyes on him. Not trusting the creature for a second. “Before we call on the Goddess to handle you like she did the second wraith.”

He gave me a glare before looking over Poppy once more, seeming to admire her tiger form. “I’ll be back.”

“Not if you plan to keep any semblance of life,” Grim said, staring at his brother in anger. Hypnos disappeared in a swirl of shadows, leaving Grim and Margaret standing on the other side of the tree. Leaving the Weavers huddled together on the porch.

As the energy around us faded, so did our bond. I no longer felt Scarlett’s hand beneath my own, and the warmth of being in their presence quickly faded. Somehow, I had lost contact with my sister. I had become shadows and death once more. Had returned fully to the Reversed and left them in the land of the living where they belonged.

Connection…severed.

CHAPTER

TWENTY-TWO

THE RISK

"Scarlett? Baby?" Shadow said, clutching his mate to his chest. "What was all that?"

"I have no idea. But I think…" Scarlett looked around, seeming confused. "I think she was here."

"Who?"

"Amber. I saw her. I *felt* her. She was here."

Shadow frowned but glanced up, looking through me even though I sat less than two feet away from him. "Yeah, this chaos seems Amber-esque."

"Jackass." I huffed, secure in the knowledge that they couldn't hear me. Poppy released a snort, though—her tiger form watching me. Almost as if she could still see me. Which had to be impossible, right? Of course, the woman had just shifted into a tiger made solely of water and flames. It seemed nothing was impossible in regard to her.

I brought a singed finger to my mouth and pursed my lips behind it, keeping my eyes on that tiger's. "Don't tell your dad I called him that."

Poppy's tiger chuffed and turned, focusing on her mother once more and leaving me to my lonesome. Well, not entirely. A pair of undead demigods stood across what was left of the yard, almost as if they were waiting for me. And perhaps they were.

I slowly rose to my feet, wishing for another moment with my sister. Knowing that wasn't possible but wanting it anyway. The cards shifted and spun, showing me Scarlett safely running along the water's edge. Showing me her future secured. A gift from the Goddess and the elements. A gift I would eventually need to repay, but one I would take comfort in. For now.

Feeling that it was time to leave my family to their own devices, I stumbled down the stairs and over the fallen tree, heading straight for Grim and Margaret. The woman caught my attention first.

"Can you talk to them?" she asked, still staring over my shoulder at the ones left on the porch. "I heard you say something—will they hear you if you speak?"

I glanced over my shoulder, catching Poppy's tiger eye. Feeling her looking directly at me again. "Not usually, but…I think so."

"He knows my mate. Tell him—tell them…" She licked her lips, her eyes going glassy. Tears obviously ready to fall. "Tell Sandman I'm still here, and I still see him."

Margaret's pain encircled me, making my chest grow tight. I'd met my red thread after our connection had been severed so I hadn't felt the attraction to him, but my sisters had found their mates in wolf shifters. I had watched their bond explode and tie the two lovers together. I couldn't imagine the absolute agony of finding that love then losing it to death. Couldn't fathom an existence without—

Grim caught my eye, his harsh features and imposing presence stealing my focus for a moment. He stood just a few feet away, watching me with wary eyes. Something in his expression called to me, spoke to the place inside me where the red thread had been severed. I brought my hand up to rub my chest without thought, needing to feel something besides emptiness there. Grim mimicked me, running a hand over his own chest as if he could feel me. Could feel my soul alongside whatever was left of his.

No man was born without a soul—not even the Grim Reaper.

Wanting to help Margaret however I could, I caught the eye of Poppy. My niece looked the two of us over before offering a quick head nod.

Message received. She really was quite the witch.

"Tell your dad," I called. "He'll know who to reach out to."

Poppy nodded again before turning to her parents. The two soul mates had been whispering something that I wasn't meant to be a part of, both wrapped up in the other. The tiger bumped her head against them, still guarding them. The child caring for the adults.

Margaret grabbed my hand—the good one—bringing me back to the present. Back to my reality.

"Thank you," she said, looking far happier than I'd ever seen her. "That's all I could have wanted."

"Thank you for fighting to save my sister. So, it wasn't you who bit me."

"No," she said with a laugh. "A simple bite is a slow way to dissolve a soul, and I don't like to play with my food. My sister, though…"

Ah. Sisters. “Yeah, I have a couple of those myself.”

She laughed and squeezed my hand, glancing at Grim. “I’m going to get back to work. You two... be careful.”

I was left alone with Grim, who appeared exhausted and battle-worn. Black ooze dripped from cuts along his arms and face, and his clothes were torn in too many places to count. The man looked as if he’d fought hard. For me and my family. That knowledge felt far more appealing than I would have liked.

“You were in a fight,” I said, sticking to the obvious. Ignoring the way my body wanted to melt into him.

“Hypnos wanted to cause more trouble than your sister was already in.”

“I figured.” I reached for his arm, my brow furrowing. “Can I—”

“Don’t.” He pulled away, almost turning sideways to keep me from touching him. “The stuff...my blood...it’s not good for you.”

But a whisper in my ear, the voice of an ancestor, told me otherwise. Eyes locked on his, I reached for his damaged arm with my hand that still glowed from within with the fire of my sister. Slowly, carefully, I traced a slice with a fingertip, cauterizing the wound. Healing him.

"How did you do that?" he asked, staring at the slight scar that had formed.

I shrugged. "My sister's ability to control fire is now within me. She's the most talented witch I ever knew. Well, she was until I saw her daughter in action. *That's* a powerful witch."

Grim twisted his arm, running a finger over the embers in my wrist. "You are so much more powerful than her."

"You're wrong, but thank you." I shivered as he caressed my wrist again, wanting so much to look into the future to see what was about to happen but fighting the urge. Letting my future roll out as it was intended to instead of manipulating it.

I traced more lines, making sure to work slowly and carefully. Learning my new gift as I dove headfirst into the conversation we needed to have. “You should have told me my soul was being devoured.”

“I wouldn’t have let it happen.”

I shook my head, my eyes on the mottled skin of my arm. “You couldn’t have stopped it.”

“I could have brought you back to your Summerlands. That would have stopped it.”

“Why didn’t you?”

“You were on a mission to save your sister. I wanted you to know she was safe first.”

I sighed, dropping my head. “She wasn’t even in danger. The cards showed me she was because I made the decision to come through the door. This whole trip was based on my desire to explore.”

He loomed over me, bringing his body closer to mine. “Because you felt me watching you. You were called to me.”

I met his gaze and raised my eyebrows. "Don't be ridiculous."

He placed a hand over his chest then one over mine, linking us where our red threads would have been. Where mine hung tattered and useless…and warm. So very warm.

"We don't need the beating or the threads or anything else," he said. "You feel me, I feel you. Anything else is excessive."

I laughed. How could I not? The man was nothing if not sure of himself. "Fine. It's your fault I made the decision to come through the door."

"I'll accept that along with any punishment you choose to dole out." He leaned closer again, deepening his voice as he said, "You have more you want to know. Ask me."

Oh, the man was right about that. I did have a lot I needed to know, so much I wanted to understand. I had felt betrayed by him more than once along the way, and it was time to know the truth about what had happened.

“Why didn’t you tell me Hypnos was your brother?”

He paused, standing stock-still before releasing a breath I knew he didn’t need. “He’s not—at least, not like you have sisters. Hypnos and I are similar but not family.”

“You should have told me about him. And you.” I flipped my arm over, showing him the scars from the bite. The black lines glowing as the embers continued to burn beneath the skin. “And this.”

Grim twisted his hand and grabbed my wrist, tugging me closer. Bringing my damaged skin to his mouth to kiss the bite and the burns. One soft, sweet press of his lips to my skin while he kept his eyes locked on mine. The man could have made my long-dead heart beat again with that look.

When his lips left my skin, they dropped into a small frown. “I didn’t want you to be afraid of me.”

The grit in his voice ran up and down my spine, making me shiver again. "I've always been afraid of you."

He yanked me closer, wrapping an arm around my hips as he murmured, "Not when you were riding my cock."

"Even then." I grinned up at him, setting both hands against his chest. "But that was fun fear."

He chuckled, the sound almost unnatural coming from him. I gave in to my desires and stepped into his hold, tucking my head against his chest and feeling the weight of his arms slip around me. He sighed once he had a good hold on me.

"That's my little witch," he said, squeezing me tight. "I enjoyed watching you and your sister work your magick—your connection is palpable."

I glanced over his shoulder at the family still on the porch, at the red and black hair of my beloved sister. At the tiger face of her daughter as she watched me. As she overheard our conversation. As she learned more about her aunt Amber than she probably wanted to know.

"We're close," I said, smiling toward my niece.

The family of three rose to their feet at that moment and began to move inside. Shadow supported my sister, and Poppy walked slightly behind. Still in tiger form. Still appearing to be on guard. Before they entered the house, she gave me one last look. A slight chuffing sound came from her throat, one I didn't recognize but that sounded positive. I shot her a smile and stared after them until the door closed. Until there was once more a physical barrier between me and my family.

The loss hit me hard, and I shivered in Grim's arms.

"What's wrong?" he asked, sounding concerned and yet mean. Ready to fight again, it would seem.

"I'm going to miss them."

"What can I do?"

I sighed, finally looking away from the house. "Tell me more about your family here."

"Hypnos and I are not family—not really. Margaret and Caoimhe weren't either. None of us was related even though they were called sisters and Hypnos is considered my brother. We are brought into *roles* here, not into families."

"And what is your role?"

"I shuttle lost souls from this undead land to their final place of rest."

"No devouring?"

"That's not my job."

As if devourer of souls was somehow a job description. Which…I suppose it was in some ways. "And do you kill people?"

"No. That's more Hypnos and Caoimhe. They're the ones taking the lives of the ones who might have lived without their…interference."

I hated Hypnos even more. "And Margaret?"

"She is a good one—she offers a quiet death to those suffering."

Oh. Ooooohhh. "She's an angel of death."

"Sort of."

"You should have told me."

He sighed again, tightening his hold on me as if afraid to let me go. "Yes, I should have."

"But you're not going to apologize."

"I was protecting you."

"I didn't need your protection."

"You actually did."

"Fine, I did. But I don't like being lied to."

"I'll never lie again."

"I will always want to know any danger that's coming my way."

"Understood." He pulled back, staring down at me. Those changing eyes burning bright blue as they met mine. "I can't promise that I won't try to shield you."

"A shield is fine, but I am my own sword. Don't force me to sheathe my powers just because you think you can fight better than I can."

"You are a better fighter than I."

"Of course I am. I'm a daughter of the Weaver line of magick." My smile fell, and I steeled myself for the next statement I knew I needed to make. The next line in the sand that had to be drawn. "I want to go home."

He froze, looking very confused. "You don't want to stay here? Close to your sister?"

"I belong in the Summerlands," I said, the truth hitting him like a physical blow. The words obviously so very painful to him. He moved to turn away, but I placed a hand on his cheek to stop him. "So, we've got a three-day walk to figure out how to make it work."

"How to make what work?" he asked, his voice grumbly and disappointed. Silly demon.

"Us."

He scoffed loudly. "With you in the Summerlands and me here."

"Yes. If Hades and Persephone could do it, so can we."

"I am no Hades, and this isn't the Underworld."

"Might as well be."

Grim shook his head, staring down at me. Those eyes so very cunning and sharp. "I can never be reincarnated."

I shrugged. "Maybe, maybe not. Doesn't matter."

"You can."

"I can…when I'm ready to be. And right now, I'm not ready to go back to the living realm." I stepped closer, biting my lower lip as I lifted up on the balls of my feet to better reach him. As I tugged him down so I could press a soft, sweet kiss to his lips. "I'm not ready to leave you behind."

He sighed against me, deepening our kiss for a moment. His hands making rough passes along my back and over my ass. Relearning me.

Reclaiming me, too. When he broke the kiss, he stared down at me for a long moment before whispering a soft, "You're sure?"

"Yeah."

A quick nod was all I got in response before he had me up and in his arms, his lips on mine and his body hard against me. He walked us into the woods before stopping against a tree. Before pressing me into the bark and writhing in that way that made me groan.

"So," he started as he moved the kiss from my lips to my neck. "How much time do I have before we start walking?"

I looked over his shoulder to the porch where Scarlett and her family had been standing. They were no longer there, retreating into the house and back to their normal lives. But I knew—I saw. My sister had felt my presence, and her grief at our time lost had matched my own. I could see her again in the cards, could feel a touch of her soul in my arm. There was no need to stay.

"Let's get off this island. I want to be alone with you."

Grim nodded, hurrying to grab my rucksack from where I'd left it before rejoining me. I ran a single finger over the singed fabric where the owl had once been and smiled, knowing the bag had served its purpose. The magick inside of it wasn't depleted—there were still trinkets and tools that lay within—but the spell that had made up feathers and a beak had been exhausted. My owl had done its job well.

"Ready?" Grim asked, watching me as I stared at that bag on his shoulder. Deep eyes locked and questioning.

I gave him a nod and tore my eyes away from the old bag, letting him carry it this time. Allowing the Reaper to relieve my burden.

Grim adjusted his hold on the bag, tossed an arm around my shoulders, and walked us toward the road. Keeping us connected as he began the journey back to the ice bridge. The Reversed was a dangerous world filled with creatures and things I knew nothing about, but Grim did. He would keep me safe. He would take care of me.

So long as I had him by my side, we would be okay.

.

.

.

Well, him and my magick. No way was I giving *that* up.

EPILOGUE

THE REWARD

The Hades and Persephone split—a few months together and a few months apart—didn't work for my Grim Reaper. It didn't work for me either, if I was being honest. Too many weeks without each other left us both anxious and cranky, so we developed a split that was more ideal. Two weeks apart with me in the Summerlands, two weeks with both of us in the Reversed. He kept me away from any sort of dangerous overpasses or death wraiths while there, but Margaret would always come around to chat and keep an eye out so we could…be distracted. I had a feeling she liked the company too. Her sadness, her palpable grief over her own death and losing her mate, was something I felt from her but couldn't even fathom. I missed my sisters terribly, but Margaret was drowning in pain and loss.

And then there was Hypnos.

"I want to see her."

The irritating demigod was the first thing I saw when I walked through the door that Grim kept open between his world and mine. The door that followed me around so he could keep an eye on me. So he could watch me. The creeper. Usually when I came through, Grim stood right there to swoop me into his arms and kiss away the long hours of separation. This time, I got Hypnos.

"No." I pushed past him, looking over the dead and smoky landscape for my love. "Where is Grim?"

"Doing his job."

Which meant someone had died and he needed to assist them from the land of the living, through the Reversed, and into their afterlife. An admirable job for sure and one people had gotten wrong for centuries. My Grim Reaper was feared in human folk stories and traditions, yet he was nothing more than a guide to help a lost soul find their forever peace. It was Hypnos and the now-dead Keres sister—the ones who literally took souls and ripped them from their bodies—that people needed to worry about. Alas, their stories had gotten buried over time. Their jobs tucked away and forgotten about. So the living feared my love instead.

"You have been blocking me, witch."

I nearly rolled my eyes. "I am not powerful enough to block you, jackass. That's all Poppy. She doesn't want you near her."

"You lie."

"And you covet what you can't have."

He looked ready to strike, ready to ignore the commands Grim had laid on him to keep me safe in the Reversed, when my own demon came rushing through the trees with a dark and smoky wolf at his side.

“Get away from her.” Grim shoved past Hypnos and grabbed me, tucking me behind him. “You know the rules.”

“She’s blocking me from Poppy.”

But Grim knew better than to believe his brother in death. “Are you blocking him, my love?”

“Nope.” You had better believe I popped that P.

“Done,” Grim said, refusing to give up even an inch to Hypnos. “Stop bothering her about this.”

Hypnos grumbled under his breath then left in a huff, dissolving into smoke and flying off into the sky. Once gone, Grim spun me around and laid a huge kiss on me, reaching to lift me off the ground by grabbing my ass and tugging me against him. This had become my favorite moment—that second of reconnection. That moment of complete loss of control as we reunited.

I couldn't hold back my grin when we broke apart. "Miss me, my demon?"

"Of course. Did you miss me, little witch?"

"Always."

He grabbed my hand—the damaged one that still glinted and glowed with hidden embers in the Reversed though looked completely normal in the Summerlands—and kissed each fingertip. Showing his love for even my broken bits. He always did that. Always paid homage to how we came together.

But I had a bigger job today than normal. "Where's Margaret?"

The wolf appeared from the tree line, shifting human to stand before me with a small, confused smile on her pretty face. "Yes?"

"I have a gift coming for you."

Margaret shot a confused look to Grim, who definitely didn't have the answers. "A gift?"

"My niece got a message to your Sandman, which started a whole chain of events back in the land of the living. I thought you might like to hear from him, too."

She gasped and nearly stumbled back, her hand flying up to her chest. "Sandman has a message for me?"

"Of course. He's your mate, and he misses you so much." At that moment, a beam of light appeared, shining down on a patch of grass across the meadow. A woman appeared between one blink and the next, looking asleep or dead. Looking so familiar it hurt. Her eyes opened slowly, her body waking up.

When she finally rose to a sitting position and glanced around, her eyes met mine, and she smiled. "Amber. It's so good to see you."

"Thanks for coming, Aoife. I assume your mate is keeping your body safe in the other realm?"

"My mate, his security team staff, half of the Feral Breed—you know, the norm."

I laughed, the overprotectiveness of wolf shifters when it came to their mates something I remembered well from both my sisters' stories.

"Aoife, I'd like you to meet Margaret, Sandman's mate."

Margaret stepped forward, looking completely shocked. "You can…come here?"

"I'm a necromancer. I can spend a little time here, but it's difficult." She held up her hand, showing a swatch on her palm that glowed red against the gray skin her form took in this realm. "My own wolf shifter mate bleeds for my protection, so I can't stay long."

I nodded when Margaret glanced my way. "This is for you. Whatever you want to say."

Aoife and Margaret spent a good amount of time sitting together, Margaret talking and Aoife writing on what looked like a rolled-up piece of tanned skin. I didn't ask—death witches and necromancers who practiced blood magick still creeped me out. Even though I *was* dead.

"Are you happy, my little witch?" Grim asked, kissing my fingertips as I leaned against his chest.

I snuggled closer to him and sighed. “I am. I miss you when we’re not together, but the reunions are so sweet.”

“Very.” He tugged me until I turned, leaning over to kiss me deeply, making my toes curl. “Speaking of sweet, the second we release the death witch back to her realm, I want to get my lips on every part of you.”

I laughed and shook my head. “Charming, aren’t you?”

“Yes. I will charm you right out of that sexy dress you’re wearing.”

By sexy, he meant long and flowy, like the skirt I’d worn when I first came through. He liked to talk about the femininity of them, but I had a feeling he was a bigger fan of the easy access they offered. Which was fine with me. It had been a long two weeks, and I needed my demigod.

Aoife and Margaret suddenly rose to their feet, offering each other a quick hug before heading our way.

“All done, then?” I asked, smiling up at the two.

Aoife nodded. "I have a lot of notes to bring back with me. Before I go, though, is there anything else? Any messages you want me to send?"

I gave that a lot of thought, knowing meddling in the world of the living could cause more problems than it solved. But there were a few things that needed to be said.

"Tell Percy I'm sorry for sending him a message the way I did."

Aoife laughed. "He told me about that. You knocked him right off his feet."

I shrugged, chagrined. "Well…I mean…it was important."

"He knows that, and he forgives you. Anything else you want me to bring back?"

Grim held tight to my hand, silent and strong behind me. Supporting me as my heart broke once again for the loss of my time with my sisters. But my life was in the afterlife. And I wouldn't give him up for anything.

I thought about all the things I could have said, all the words I once would have wanted to say. And then I ignored 95% of them.

"Tell Poppy to guard herself against Hypnos. He won't stop coming for her." I sighed, silent for a long moment as I remembered that day at the Mackinac Island house. "And tell Scarlett and Azurine that I miss them both every day, but that I'm happy. Tell them if they feel a cold wind across their cheek on a summer day, that's just me saying hi."

Aoife gave me a soft smile before looking toward Grim. "Take care of her for us."

Grim squeezed me tight. "Always."

And he would. I knew it. I may have once misunderstood the man, but I had learned so much about him since then. I knew his softness and how much he cared for me, knew his strength and how he would fight for me. I knew that, so long as we kept our connection strong, we would find a way to be together. Living in two realms of existence couldn't stop us because we would find a way to be together. We would figure out how to stand by each other's side.

Death was not the end.

Not for us.

About the Author

A storyteller from the time she could talk, Ellis grew up among family legends of hauntings, psychics, and love spanning decades. Those stories didn't always have the happiest of endings, so they inspired her to write about real life, real love, and the difficulties therein. From farmers to werewolves, store clerks to witches—if there's love to be found, she'll write about it. Ellis lives in the Chicago area with her two daughters and a German Shepherd that never leaves her side.

When she's not writing paranormal romance, Ellis Leigh can be found writing romantic suspense as Kristin Harte and erotic shorts as London Hale.

www.ingramcontent.com/pod-product-compliance
Lightning Source LLC
Chambersburg PA
CBHW030628310726
48979CB00003B/925

* 9 7 8 1 9 5 4 7 0 2 3 2 5 *